Ir

by

Celinda Labrousse

This is a work of fiction. Names, characters, places, and incidents are products of the author's imagination or are used fictitiously and are not to be mixed up with anything that is real. Any resemblance to actual events locales, organizations, or persons, living or dead, is entirely coincidental.

IMPERIAL EDGE Copyright 2020 by Celinda Labrousse. All rights reversed. All rights reserved under International and Pan-American Copyright conventions. By payment of the required fees, you have been granted the nonexclusive, nontransferable right to access and read the text of this ebook on screen. No part of this text may be reproduced, transmitted, downloaded, decompiled, reverse-engineered, or stored in or introduced into any information storage and retrieval system, in any form or by any means, whether electronic or mechanical, now known or hereafter invented, without the express written permission of the publisher.

Digital Edition 2020

ISBN 9798622910708

Cover art by Karri Klawiter

Published by Labrousse Enterprises

All rights reserved

To Jessica finally one you can read ;-)

Chapter 1

Chapter 2

Chapter 3

Chapter 4

Chapter 5

Chapter 6

Chapter 7

Chapter 8

Chapter 9

Chapter 10

Chapter 11

Chapter 12

Chapter 13

Chapter 14

Chapter 15

Chapter 16

Chapter 17

Chapter 18

Author's Note

Preview: Imperial HIlt (Book 2 in Miranda's saga)

Chapter 1

Breakfast was served in the kitchen. The press cook stove, a hold over from three generations back, still managed to pump out usable heat, even though the thing was held together with duct tape and prayers. The button to the oven door had to be pushed at just the right angle or it would fall off. Then the whole thing would have to cool down before the handle could be reattached. That's why most of the morning's fixins lay scattered in different dishes across the top burners.

Thinly sliced ors butt in one pan. Baking beans in another. Plus who could forget the pancakes. The fluffy mix of water and fresh ground wheat that was the staple crop of Oreilly 13 smelled no less appetizing this morning than every morning of Miranda's 17 years.

"Can you take over for me, sweetie?" asked her mom as she floated towards the warm pile of pancakes stacked high by the stove.

"Sure," said Miranda. Miranda's mom was a stout woman. Strong arms that could lift a large stack of pancakes in one hand and a plate overflowing with ors butt in the other. Both of which she carried over to the table where the kids were all lined up in a row. Michael rounded the corner, ending the line of forks and knives ready to devour the feast.

Miranda poured another dollop of dough into the pan. It sizzled on contact. She smiled, watching the cooking batter with one eye and her family eating everything in sight with the other.

"What are you all doing here today?" Miranda asked her older brother Micah. It was a rarity to see him, his wife, and their brood. The trek from town where they lived to the homestead was long.

"Anna drove us since I got off shift last night," Micah said, giving his wife a shoulder hug. I forced a smile to my face.

"Your dad called me yesterday morning. Said the harvest was coming in quicker than he'd anticipated." It was dangerous asking for help with harvest. A second crew could mean an extra toll cost. But Michael was too short to reach the second turbine controls and I had my hands full with the animals now that Mary Ann was married. As the eldest Micah would inherit the farm, so by calling him Dad was walking a fine line. Micah was family, not a worker, so the tax might be bypassed. Maybe.

"Must be some crop," Mom replied. The controlled expression on her face said that she hadn't known Dad had called in reinforcements either. Interesting.

"Don't know until I get out there today," Micah said through mouthfuls of syrup-drenched fluff. "All I know for sure is that he thinks it will all go up in smoke if isn't in by tomorrow."

All the eating came to a screeching halt. Harvest fires were no joke on Oreilly 13. They destroyed more than the crops. Some could wipe out a barn full of livestock and keep going. They spread like plague across farms, devastating whole farmsteads. People died.

"If Dad thinks there's going to be a fire..." Miranda started to say.

"Better to be wary," Micah said, shoving another mound of pancakes into his mouth. The chorus of forks and knives on plates resumed. Fire changed everything. The extra tax would be worth it. Even if we couldn't get it all in, there would be less to burn around the house and spread to our neighbors.

"Won't the Ironsides save us?" Michael piped up.

"From fire?" Mary yawned. "Not very likely." Micah shot her a hard look.

"But my vid lesson this week said that Ironsides are here to protect us from everything!" Michael informed us all. Mother and I stifled a laugh. Those vid programs made Ironsides out to be superheroes. Every boy and girl from the outer galaxies wanted to be one. It's why second sons like Michael often ended up in the military.

"Ironsides keep the planet safe from rebels and invading forces. They don't really take care of planetary fires," Mary corrected.

"But the vid said..." Michael started to say.

"Who wants more pancakes?" Mom interrupted, cutting off the conversation. Every little hand went up. Soon the plate sat empty beside Miranda, ready for the batch she'd just finished cooking up. She flipped them out onto the plate and poured the last of the batter onto the griddle stone.

"Here, I can take it back over if you want to eat," Mom said, going to take up her place by the stove. Miranda scooted past her, intent on filling her plate to overflowing. This would likely be the only hot meal of the day. All hands on deck to bring the harvest in. No wonder Dad was already out in the fields. He was probably laying down fire breaks to minimise the possibility of damage if a blaze caught early.

She would have her hands full wrangling in the livestock with Mother.

"I'm off," Micah proclaimed. He kissed the tops of his three kids' heads as he made his way down the table towards the door. "No time like the present." He stopped long enough to kiss Anna on the cheek. "Get some rest sweetheart. You deserve it after that drive." She smiled back at him. It was a tired smile with dreams of a soft bed and a pillow in its future.

"Where's Oscar?" Micah asked. Michael and Morgan stared hard down into their plates.

"What did you two do now?" Miranda scolded them. Her hands migrated naturally to her hips. It was the stance Mary Ann use to take with her when she'd gone and done something she didn't want anyone to know about.

"Leave me out of this," Micah said, stepping out the door and into the morning sun. The door swung shut behind him with a clang.

"Me too," said Anna. "I'm to bed. Micah, you watch over your sister Anna and mind what Grandma Mary tells you, you hear?" The two oldest nodded their heads.

"Mary, it's been nice seeing you. When I wake up and this settles down, I'll be happy to catch up." Anna pulled away from the table, her blue cotton dress falling neatly back over her knees all the way to her ankles. Anna was all the way up the stairs when Miranda turned on her two younger siblings.

"Answer the question," she said. The two looked at each other, looked at Miranda, then proceeded to stare at the floor. Their faces glued to spots only they could see.

"Out with it," Miranda barked. Michael winced.

"It's not our fault, honest," Morgan caved first. "I closed the door after I came in I swear."

"Yeah, I saw her latch it and everything," Michael chimed in. "The stupid piece of junk done popped the door open and run out before either of us could get to the bottom of the stairs."

"Michael you watch your tongue. I wouldn't have such language in my house!" Mom scolded him.

"How long has he been missing?" Miranda said, moving her hands from her hips to her temples. She could feel a headache coming on.

"Since before Mom started frying the ors butt."

Morgan started snickering. Something about the word butt always gave her the giggles.

"You mean to tell me that Oscar has at least an hour, if not two, head start, and you didn't think to tell any of us this?" Miranda confirmed.

"Well I just…" Michael started to say.

At the same time, Morgan said, "Yes, but we were hungry."

"And what? You think we would have sent you out looking for him and that you would have missed breakfast?" Miranda asked, hands firmly back on hips.

"Yeah," they chorused.

"You can't beat their logic," Micah the Third added from his seat in the middle.

"I wasn't asking you," Miranda said, "I was asking them." She stared down both of them, each with an extra stink eye. Miranda looked over at her mother.

"They will do all your chores while you're gone," Mom said. Miranda wanted to argue. To tell her that the family would be much better off without the stupid escape-artist robot. That as small kids her brother and sister could track the thing better than she could. Nothing came out of her mouth. It hung open for the moment, then closed of its own accord.

"I better get a move on then," said Miranda.

"Yes," Mom said.

Miranda stuck a fork in the top of the pancake pile and shoved the thing into her mouth and trudged out the door. She was too hungry not to have breakfast. Plus what good would it do the family to find Oscar if she just lost him again because she passed out from hunger? She stepped out onto the porch, desperate for any sign of the disobedient robot. Something on the edge of the field flashed, blinding her. She raised her hand to shield her eyes and sighed through her mouth of pancake. This was going to be one long day.

Chapter 2

MIRANDA CURSED HER sister. Mary Ann had left for her own homestead in the Parsol system as soon as she turned eighteen leaving Miranda to rangle up the droid when it made it's monthly run for the hills.

"Oscar! Oh, Oscar!" she called. She'd picked up the droid's trail not too far from the house. The bot had no camo-unit functions so it left a track you could drive a hoverboard through. Not that Miranda owned a hoverboard. There was an old hoverbike in pieces in the garage. Her eldest brother Micah had pulled the thing apart to fix it and never got the parts to fit back together. Dad was always talking about selling the thing, but he never did. Her family was way too nostalgic. Hence why she was tracking an old piece of junk past the homestead boundary and into the outer forest. The thing wasn't even worth the half day of work she was missing, but her hide was worth it. So were her ears. Her mother would have both if she walked back through the front door without Oscar.

She followed the path up off the grassy plain and into the tree edge at the base of the valley floor. It continued into the forest. If his goal was to lose her then he was making all the right moves.

"Oscar, you stupid robot; get back here!" she yelled. Nothing. No squeaky wheels or obscene beeping. The droid was truly good and lost.

"This is going to take up a whole day," she told the trees. Then she heard it.

It started out as a buzzing sound low and far away. Then it grew until it was a roar right above her head. That noise certainly wasn't Oscar. She looked up in the general direction it was coming from. A black spot marked something flying in the sky casting a shadow through the trees. It was a hovercraft; black, with a large oval body and tiny tiny wings. The trees limited her view of it, but the noise that it made marked it as one of the old S series models that firefighters and low ranking government officials used to travel around the planet.

Dad had been right. If it was the fire brigade coming out this far, the fields where burning somewhere and we had very little time to pull in the crop and ready the farm. Fire flyovers meant evacuations. If Oscar stayed out without a family member it would for sure be picked up by a reclaim bot and upcycled for parts. Or worse, melted down. Miranda quickened her pace.

For being an old piece of junk Oscar sure could move fast when he wanted to. Not two hours gone and the thing was far enough away that Miranda couldn't see the house anymore.

"Stupid, stupid, stupid bot!" she yelled at the tracks in front of her. She tripped on a tree root, taking a tumble into a bramble bush. Thorns scraped her arms and clung to her dress. She didn't like the blue thing all that much, but she didn't want patches on it either.

"Stupid droid!" she screamed. Maybe if it heard her it would feel bad and come back. The incline was growing steeper by the minute. The trees thinned out as the air dipped below breathable levels.

"Oscar!" Miranda yelled. The word echoed off the rocks. Miranda's mother Mary had named the stupid thing when she had gotten it off a caravan trader at the planetary fair back when she was a little girl.

"The bot's first-generation tech," Miranda recited from memory. Which of course was a bunch of ors pucks, but Miranda's mom had been eight and in love with everything Lander at the time. Even getting to trade with an offworlder was a huge thing for a girl of eight. She gave up two woven bolts of the finest spun silk for the worthless excuse of a droid.

Oreilly 13 was a harvest planet, colonised for food production. All mountain ranges and fertile valleys. People in the capital planet of Creche needed food. Given that the entire planet had become a kind of city with middle and upper tiers, it was no wonder the empire seeded planets on the outer rims like Dad sowed wheat. Oreilly 13 was a third-generation seedling, the governments and towns just starting to have on-world trade. The silk was one of the few goods offworlders valued. Heavy tolls on the wheat kept prices down. Sure, some farmers provided meats like sheep and ors. Ors being the most common. Both were imports after the planet was colonized. But there were rare occasions when they took to a planet's terraforming and made it their own.

Miranda amused herself by trying to remember all the rules to farm steaders. On a first generation seed planet, it was different. You had your family and that was it. Oreilly 13 was in its third generation so it made the laws harder. Only a male could inherit. Either a son or a son-in-law. You had to be married when your father passed away. No single person could get a farm. It took a brood to keep a homestead operational and the Empire did not wish for its subjects to fail to produce.

Miranda was so deep into her thoughts that she missed the edge of the ravine and went toppling over. Down she fell, end over end. Her head, shoulder and back bounced off the side of the ravine until she found herself on a shelf. Her butt hit something hard.

Tears stung her eyes, but at least she wasn't falling anymore.

"Oscar, you stupid robot! Why'd you have to run off so far? Dad said that there might be fire. Fire! And now I've fallen down this ravine. So someone will have to stop prepwork and bringing in the harvest to come and haul me out of this stupid place, all because of you!" Her words echoed off the walls bouncing their harsh tones back at her.

"Stupid place, stupid place" the walls replied. The sun overhead had begun to dip down. How long would it take them to track her beacon? She'd been walking for at least six hours before her fall. On the family hovercraft it would take maybe forty minutes. But the hover cart couldn't trek through the forest, so they would probably send Mom or Miranda's sister-in-law out with a wedger. Those things weren't as reliable as a good hover engine, but they got the job done. At max she'd be down here an hour and then they would be hauling her out and scolding her for getting lost trying to find a lost droid.

"You'll never live this down," she told the walls.

"You'll never, you'll never, you'll never" her voice echoed back. On the inside wrist of her arm lay a small button-like bulge that acted as a beacon. It would relay a distress signal back to her family. Better to have a dinner story than to die of dehydration and pride. She hit the tracking button. And waited.

Miranda sighed. It was more than falling, than getting lost. She'd failed to retrieve Oscar. There was no chasing it farther up the mountain. Not without a true search crew, and no droid was worth that. The droid was truly lost this time. Nothing she could say or do would change that.

Time passed. The sun slid from right above her to behind the edge of the ravine, covering her in a blanket of darkness. It wasn't pitch black. But it would make it harder for her family to find her. Why weren't they here yet?

Even if they'd sent the kids walking with a laser tether they would have been within calling distance by now. Miranda was perplexed.

She stood up and began to pace. What was taking them so long? Didn't they know that she was helpless? Was the possi-

IMPERIAL EDGE

bility of fire shifted to real fire? Maybe they'd had to evacuate and in the rush forgot that she was out there.

Miranda's heart started to thump rapidly in her chest. There was no way they could have forgotten about her, right? She wasn't so sure anymore. Maybe they were all dead and no one was coming for her.

"No," she told herself. "You cannot think such gruesome thoughts."

"Bee bi bi bop boo boop bap," came a noise from under her.

"That's what I just said. I can't think of such gruesome thoughts!"

Miranda paused. The rock she had landed on when she rolled into the ledge was beeping at her. She picked the baby sized thing up and rubbed off the dirt with a corner of her dress. Shiny metal and buttons looked back at her.

"Oscar!" she cried.

"Oscar, Oscar, Osscaarrrr," the walls echoed.

"You stupid, stupid droid." She couldn't believe how happy she was to see the little monstrosity.

"Bee bop booo-p," it told her back.

"Yes, you are stupid. Running away like that."

"Bee bee bee boop," Oscar responded.

"No, I'm not making a mountain out of an ors' pile," Miranda confirmed, "you got us stuck in a ravine."

"Beep beep boop."

"I get that life on the farm can get boring, but this is not an adventure, not a good one anyway," she told the little droid.

"Beep beep beeeep."

"'Why not?'" Miranda sputtered to find an answer. "Because. Because I'm hurt and we got stuck. And yes, I know that I should have seen this coming and saved you and then we could be on our way home right now, but I didn't and we can't get out of here. That's why not!" Miranda rubbed her arms with her palms. It was getting cold this high on the mountain without the sun on her. Soon it would be night and then getting out of this place would become twice as hard. She had to take control. For whatever reason rescue wasn't coming. She would have to contend herself with getting out of this hole and then finding her way back home.

She just needed to think. Oscar might be old, but he wasn't a completely useless droid. Miranda pressed a few buttons and voila! A side panel popped out, exposing a drop cutter. She angled it into the side of the ravine and fired. A beam of light cut into the side of the mountain.

"Beep bo beep!" the droid complained.

"Yes I know it's going to drain your battery, but you can recharge in the morning." she told the cantankerous droid. He was solar powered, so all he needed was a few good hours sunbathing to get back up to full power.

She stepped out and onto the newly formed stair she'd carved from the side of the rock. Once she was settled she fired again. Fire. Step. Fire. Step. On and on it went until she was at last out of the ravine. The sun crested the top of the mountain. Dark would fall for real in a couple of hours. She had just enough time to find shelter.

Droid in hand she trudged down the mountain, all thoughts of her missing rescuers shoved far into the back of her brain. She had a shelter to find or build and drive to return home.

Chapter 3

Everything ached. Her feet ached from the hike up the mountain. Her back ached from spending the night sleeping on the forest floor. Her arms ached from carrying the droid. Her head and side ached from falling into the ravine. It was so bad she couldn't pinpoint any one pain. It was just a big ball of ouch from the crown of her head to the bruised tips of her toes. All because a little droid wanted to have a big adventure.

Miranda sighed.

"You need to start getting your priorities straight," she told Oscar. "You are too old to be constantly running off. Little Michael still loves games. He has that fort in the woods where he battles rebels for the Empire. You could be his attack droid."

"Beep beep boop," the little monster cut in.

"No, imagining can be just as fun as the real thing," she continued to say as they trudged through the wood. She could see the edge of their fields just up ahead. It was still a two or three hour walk, but at least she would be free of the gloom of the woods. The sun was still in early morning formation so the heat wouldn't be that bad.

"Imagining means you can turn the wood into another planet and not have to travel galaxies to get back home for lunch," she said.

"Bee boop," agreed the droid. Miranda's stomach had stopped growling last night and sat unhappily empty. She would be starving, but the thirst was worse. Her tongue had an unpleasant patina of grime that her saliva glands could not produce enough to get rid of. She hadn't needed to pee since waking up.

"That's the first sign of dehydration," she said to Oscar. When you imagine something like Mom's lemonade was just a hop skip and a jump away. She imagined that lemonade in her mind. The tartness of the fruit mixed with real sugar. It all came out of the ration cans the Empire sent as thank yous for paid tributes. Mom would prepare it for Dad during harvest or for the kids when they were dehydrated from adventuring. "Better than water to rehydrate someone for hard work," Miranda said with a sigh. "That's what the can reads, anyway."

Miranda, like all Empire children, had received three hours a day of mandatory Imperial schooling vid-tapes and testing for the past several years. She knew how to read and write in both common and Imperial. She also spoke Droid. She wished that she knew the language of the people that had built Oscar. Even if she could understand what he was saying, he couldn't tell her exactly what the scratches and symbols on his body meant.

She had spent a whole season making up guesses. Finding every button and switch that he had. Fixing them up so they'd work right. She was in her scientific explorer phase. That's what Mom had called it. She meticulously wrote down every experiment, every button combination, until there was nothing left to try. Of all the family, she knew the most about Oscar. Kept it all in her notebook she carried around.

She never left home without it. One year on Planter's Day her dad had given her a brobanium necklace. It was the toughest metal in the galaxy. People made blaster guns out of it. She'd hung the notebook off of it to always keep it on her person.

She touched it now. Still there. It hadn't come off in the fall or while she slept.

Oscar beeped out a bunch of nonsensical tones.

"Yes I know you don't drink or eat, but you still need sunlight. If you fall into a hole and your battery dies you'd feel the same way I do now!" she told him. "Oh, wait. You did. And I had to come save you." He grumbled in low beeps in her arms, but didn't say anything else.

The long green branches of the trees gave way to the wheat fields stretching out for miles in front of her. She stood on the edge of the field. Her arms ached from carrying Oscar. The sweat she'd poured out had dried up. Her fingers had swollen to twice their normal size. She would start blowing tumbleweeds out of her mouth if she didn't get water soon.

"Well Oscar, we have two options," she told him. "I could let you down and you could charge your batteries in the sun for a few hours while we walk home, at which point I might pass out from lack of water and then you would have to go home and fetch someone to get me or I'd die."

"Beep beep," he responded cheerfully.

"Yes, you'd be able to go back on your adventure, but I wouldn't come after you this time because I'd be dead," she retorted.

"Beep," he asked.

"Or, we can go to the mid water hole and I could get some usable water to drink. Then we could go home. Either way I have to let you down. And if you don't promise to walk with me then I'll have to turn you off and come back for you once I've gotten water and food."

"Beep boop," replied the droid.

"Yes, I am aware that you will be unprotected if I turn you off and that if the tractor runs over you or an upcycle unit find you that would be it," she replied, her voice smooth.

"Beep beep!" Oscar said.

"No, I found you, so Mom can't be mad if it was carry you or die."

Oscar huffed through his vent holes.

"Well, I know my vote," she went for his off switch. He tried in vain to shimmy out of her arms.

"Beep, beep!" Oscar cried. Miranda blew a piece of hair out of her eyes. It had fallen loose form her braid in the struggle. She smiled, knowing she'd won.

"So we have a deal then. I put you down, you follow me to the watering hole then home."

"Beep boop," the poor dejected bot said. Miranda ignored him and trudged ahead into the field.

It was hard to see over the wheat. Her brother said it looked like a desert. The school tapes had described a desert as an ocean of earth. Miranda had never seen an ocean. There was one on the planet, of course. That's where the capital was, and some of the higher ranking Creshie that oversaw the collection of the taxes for land ownership. Her father had seen it. So had her brother. Her mother had gone with them once, to make their ten-year balancing of records.

It was the way the Empire made sure their tax collectors weren't overcharging the people. An independent auditor would check the books of the farmers against the books of the collectors to see if everything aligned. If a farmer thought to cheat the Empire they would be stripped of their land and their families would be sentenced to mining work for four generations. Whereas if a collector was caught with off books they would be hung publicly, all of their riches given to the Empire as tribute. It was important to have clean books. Ten years was a long time to keep the records. Miranda had been twelve for the last one. Too young to go. She was five years from the next one. She was more likely to see it as a married woman.

"Only time will tell," she told the grass as she ran her fingers through the long grains. Oscar stopped to stare at her. She shook herself from the daze. The rising sun and the endless field must have been entrancing her because she barely heard Oscar's warning to jump down before the tractor was upon her.

The thing was barrelling out of control. Left and right it went. Neither a straight line like her father liked to make, nor the back and forth pattern her brother preferred. It was fully out of control.

"Hey!" she called up at the driver. Nothing. "Hey!" she screamed at the driver again. The hovertrax kept harvesting, sorting and baling wheat. She ran to try and get his attention. It had to be her father or brother.

"Hey!" she said, banging on the cabin door. The vehicle swerved left away from her. She fell behind. She was so tired and out of breath. The thing shot a bale of straw at her.

She watched the craft shift away from her just fast enough that she couldn't catch it. Watched it take a wide turn following the edge of the hill. Then back over again. A snake pattern unfolded from the cut ground.

She hung her head between her knees and gulped in air. This day was getting better and better. Just when she thought she might be able to try it again, it turned a sharp right, putting her right in its path. She jumped aside and then sprinted for the cab. She got one hand on the door handle and heaved herself up into the driver compartment. Her dad lay just out of sight, slumped over the wheel.

Hot air blew through the vents. The cooling must have gone out, Miranda surmised, and Dad passed out from the heat. She stuck her hand around him and felt for the off switch.

"There," she said with satisfaction as the machine powered down and finally coasted to a stop. By then Oscar had caught up. She heaved her dad up and over onto her shoulder, then down to the ground. Then she looked around the cabin for some water. Or ever better, lemonade. His canteen was in its pocket. She grabbed it and then returned to look him over.

He was paler than usual, his skin gray. His eyes were closed and his breath was so shallow she swore it wasn't there. It was worse than she thought; he'd gone into shock. She looked down to give him chest compressions. That's when she saw it.

All exhaustion fled her. The thirst that had been driving her to the well evaporated. Her vision tunneled around her dad and the hole in his chest where his heart should be. No blood, just a black hole where flesh should be. She pounded on him, recalling the emergency resuscitation videos all kids were forced to learn before operating any of the farm's equipment.

One. Two. Three. Tilt head and breath into his mouth.

One. Two. Three. He couldn't be dead. Tears she didn't know she had the water to cry coursed down her cheeks.

One. Two. Three. She breathed into his lungs again. No air movement. No breath. He was gone. The smell finally hit her nose. The stench of rotting human flesh. He'd been dead for hours and she'd been too blind to see it.

Oscar pulled on her, dragging her away from the body. Miranda let him, not wanting to remember her father as this lifeless pile of flesh. She tripped on something, her eyes not looking where they were going. It was her dad's canteen. She was so thirsty and he wasn't going to need it. A fresh wave of tears came pouring out of her as she took a sip of the water.

It cooled her throat and brought back some of her senses.

Mom. Someone had to tell Mom. Mom would know what to do. Miranda took three long drags on the canteen until the last of the contents were gone, and then she ran as fast as her tired legs would take her back to her home.

Chapter 4

The house looked deserted. Only the wind whipping the Imperial flag on the flagpole gave off the signs that a happy family lived in this place. The white trim looked shadowed, but there wasn't a cloud in the sky. Miranda shivered. A cold not congruent with the noonday sun stiffened her back. The cold drove her forward.

"You've run this far," she told herself. "If you don't tell, how's Mom going to know about Dad?" She needed to find Mom. She raced across the porch and around the side to the kitchen entrance. The screen door clanged behind her; the only sound for miles. There was Mom. Standing by the kitchen stove. Her hand holding a cast iron skillet. The contents of which were pouring out black smoke. Miranda coughed. Covering her mouth with one sleeve, she pulled on her mother's shoulder with the other.

"Mom, your hand!" Miranda cried. She pulled her mother back from the stove. Her mother, free from the flames, collapsed at Miranda's feet. A pile of burning flesh and pink dyed cotton with daisy chains down in the hem.

"Mom!" Miranda cried again. Oscar poked the corpse, looking for life in the pile of flesh. Miranda's mother didn't stir. Miranda's mind raced. If Mom had been shot in the kitchen, where were her sisters and brothers? She raced up the stairs, hoping to find life.

She flung opened the guest room door revealing her sleeping sister-in-law.

"Wake up," Miranda screamed. "Wake up! Everyone's dead! You have to wake up." Anna lay there unmoving, as pretty as a cryo sleeper. Her eyes closed. A touch of a smile on her lips. Happy to be in a dream. Miranda pounded on Anna's chest.

"Wake up!" she cried. Miranda lifted her hands to strike the woman again only to notice that they were red. Crimson was spreading out all over the sheets. Miranda pulled the quilt aside. Anna lay in a pool of her own blood.

This wasn't a blaster fire. Anna's neck had been sliced open with a blade. She would have bled out in seconds. Never waking from her sleep.

Miranda stood there, quilt in one hand, the cold dead neck of Anna in the other. She couldn't will her mind to stop tumbling over the possibilities. Oscar had followed her up the stairs. He stood by the door, too scared to come inside.

"Beep bop," he said in a hushed tone.

"The children," she repeated.

"The children!" Her brother and sister, niece and nephew. They weren't here. Maybe, just maybe. She turned and made her way back down the stairs, not stopping to waste the blood off her hands. Each step an extension of pure will. Her body pushed to its breaking point, her mind not far behind.

As she passed through the hallway she heard a loud beeping. The sound pounded on her ears. Part of her wondered why she hadn't heard it coming up the stairs, but she chalked that up to the rushing sound in her ears. It was their tracker board. It was a map of the valley traced out in lights and other bits and pieces the family had stuck to it to make it look more three dimensional. Her emergency beacon was still transmitting her cry for help. No one had come for her. No one could come. They were all dead.

"Don't think like that," she scolded herself. There was still the children. Maybe they'd been playing and one of them escaped. And her older brother Micah. He could be protecting them all.

She shot out the door and down the super secret path back towards the base of the woods. No answer. Maybe they thought whoever did this was still here. Still out to get them if they left the safety of the forest.

A head of sandy brown hair tripped her three feet from the porch. She toppled onto the ground, dust and rocks digging into her palms.

She looked back at the body that tripped her. Her oldest brother's wide eyed stares met her gaze.

"Micah!" She scrambled to her feet. "Please God let him be alive." She knew that he wasn't. Could see it in the blank gaze of his eyes looking up at her from the dirt. As she moved closer she could guess at what he'd been doing in the last few minutes of his life.

Micah had been coming back towards the house. He was surprised by someone he wasn't expecting to see. Tried to turn around, only to get a blaster to the back of the head, sending him flying. The signs were written all around her. The kicked up dirt. The surprised expression of fear on his frozen features. The blaster mark through his back. The guessing came from why he'd been going towards the house. Had Mom screamed? Or maybe it was lunch time when this all happened. Miranda wanted to remember all the evidence.

Not that there was much to be had. This place she'd once called home felt like a cemetery. Miranda trudged on, making sure to step over her brother's body. She didn't want to disturb his peace, what little of it was left. If she touched him it would be real.

It wasn't long until she'd left the safety of the fields to the weirdness of the woods once more. Oscared followed after lowering his speaker. Better not to bring attention to themselves. They had to find the kids. They just had to.

The fort wasn't really a fort. It wasn't much of anything. At some point in its life dad had used it as a hunting bluff back when he was a boy and the farm had been plagued with wild ors. But the ors heard had long since moved on. The bluff was a tree house when her eldest brother lived with them. He would use it to get away from all the chaos, as he liked to call it. One fateful afternoon the supports had given out and the whole thing toppled to the ground. Now it was a fort. Michael had spent considerable time constructing it. Gathering random sticks and stones to shore up the sides and make it whole. It kind of grew from there into a sprawling mess of things that provided little cover, but hours of entertainment.

Branches tore at her hair and scraped her face. If the people that had killed her family were still here, they would have heard her and set up a trap. She didn't care. She just needed to find someone, anyone, alive. Her sides heaved from all the running she'd been doing as she looked over the remains of what had once been the fort.

It was a pile of smoking ash. The outline of a child blasted out of existence lay against an oak to her right. The curled up body of either her sister or her niece lay at her feet. The head was missing. There was no blood. Not even the smell of cooked meat remained. The only signs of death were the blast marks and the bodies.

She struggled into what was left of the fort, desperate for a survivor. The embers still smoked, kept alive by the summer heat. The heat cut into her boots. Black smudges covered her hands, her face, her clothes as she searched for the remaining two children. She found them huddled together. Shot to pieces by blaster fire. The ruin around them their only protection.

Miranda dropped to her knees. Uncontrollable sobs wracked her body. The ash burning holes in her dress. The pain was a small shadow to the ache that penetrated her every limb.

That's when she heard it. The soft crunch of feet on a wooded floor.

She continued to cry, but it was much more controlled. All her fear senses were screaming 'predator!' at her. They had taken her family away. They would not take her without a fight. She stood up, grabbing the nearest thing she could use for a weapon.

Dust swirled around her, landing on the edges of the air to her right. It clung to something that looked to Miranda like nothing at all. She swung. The smoldering tree branch struck gold.

The soldier was taken off guard. She hit him square in the head. If he hadn't been wearing his helmet she might have even knocked him out. She shouldn't have been able to see him. But somehow she had. His suit flickered for a minute, the controls in the helmet fighting to stay intact. Then the camo unit zapped out, revealing the Ironside in all his glory.

Miranda had read about them in school. Watched the holograms talk through all their impressive armor in agonizing detail. Colony families like hers were protected by the Ironsides. They were the backbone of the planetary troops that kept the rebels at bay. Their suits had two modes. Camo mode, which practically made them invisible; the armor actively blended the scenery around the suit into the reflection of the armor on the eyes. The second was marching whites like she was looking at now.

Miranda stepped back into a batting pose. Legs bent at the knees, arms ready to swing the branch again. Their helmets were crazy expensive and she'd just damaged his. He would be out for her blood. A reclaimed helmet could buy a farm. Not that anyone she'd known was ever close enough to a battle to reclaim one. Still, it was the dream of every farm boy she'd ever known to get to see an Ironside. A helmet reclaim was like chasing the terraformed planet at the end of the galaxy. It happened, only enough to make people dream about it.

The Ironside raised his hands in surrender.

"I'm not here to hurt you," he said. It came out garbled. His language filter device must have been damaged when she'd hit him. Those helmets were meant to take a mortal blast from a phase canon and keep moving. She must have hit it just right.

Miranda heard a click to her left and sung around. She saw nothing, but the hair on the back of her neck stood up. Someone was there. Another Ironside. She just couldn't see him.

"It's ok, Miss," said the one she'd hit. "Just put down the stick and everything will be ok."

Miranda did as she was told. She was no match for two Ironsides. Not even if she'd had a phase weapon on her. This was an Imperial farm. There were no phase weapons for miles. The closest thing they had was a laser pistol Dad used to use to kill ors. She hadn't thought to grab it when she'd went running after the kids. Now was a bit late.

As soon as the stick touched the ground the first Ironside popped off his helmet with a click.

"All clear," the soldier called. Three other Ironsides stepped out into view. They seemed to melt in the air as if appearing out of the afternoon mist.

"Rebels were spotted landing around here yesterday," the Ironside said.

"No," Miranda said, shaking her head. "There was a fire suppression craft heading south. But that was yesterday."

"Sir, bodies are at least a day old," one of the other Ironsides said.

A day old. Miranda let that knowledge sink in. If she hadn't gone after Oscar. If she hadn't gotten lost in the ravine. Would she be just another one of the bodies they were cleaning up?

"Miss, you said south?" asked her Ironside. He had black hair and blue green eyes that made his tan face look nice. Not as menacing as the cold white masks the helmet made of the others. He was the only one without his helmet on. They must really like it in those things, she thought.

"Miss." He bent low enough that they were eye to eye. She hadn't answered him. Was he worried for her? An Ironside that cared about a poor farm girl. That was the start of galactic romance novels her older sister liked to read before she went off and got married.

"Yes, south. Over the farm. Dad talked about fire coming. Pulled in my brother to help. We needed to save the farm."

The Ironside nodded.

"Who did this?" Miranda asked.

"Rebels."

"Why?" she asked.

He shrugged.

"Who knows why rebels do anything."

All the rage and fear that the shock of finding her family that way had held in check came tumbling out of her.

"If you knew they were here why didn't you protect my family?" she screamed as she pounded the one soildier's uniform.

"I'm sorry. I'm so sorry," he said into her ear he held her in a hug, letting her pound his back with empty fists until the rage and grief left her a hollow shell that crumpled to the forest floor.

"Time to move out," one of the others said.

"Is this yours?" Another soldier held up Oscar by his antenna.

"Oscar!" Miranda cried. The presence of the little pest renewed her strength. She snatched the droid out of the air and cradled him to her chest.

"I caught him trying to penetrate our defense perimeter," the soldier reported to the Ironside that had let her pound him. He looked silvery white, too, when the camo function was off. Like a mirror without an edge. It was hard to focus on any one of them.

"Time to move," her Ironside said. He let her go and slipped back in with the other troops, putting his helmet back on.

IMPERIAL EDGE

"He could report you, you know," said another Ironside. "Hitting a member of the military is a capital offense." Miranda's eyes widened. Were they really going to report her?

"Then I would have to explain to the entire command how I let a nothing of a girl land multiple strikes," he told the other Ironside. His helmet moved up and down, scanning her from top to bottom. "You're not worth it,"

Miranda's cheeks turned fiery hot. She didn know if she wanted to hide or hit the man for real this time. She gripped Oscar instead and watch the Ironsides blend back into the trees as they switched the camo graphics back onto their suits until only her Ironside remained.

"There's a transport unit back at the farm house. If you hurry you might be able to hitch a ride with them into town."

She looked at the bodies of her family.

"Cleanup crew's been called. The new farm tenants have already been assigned."

"They'll bury them?" she asked, knowing that he wouldn't have an answer. Not really.

"The bodies will be gone before nightfall. Best to get the ride. This isn't your home anymore," he said. He turned and blended into the forest with the rest of his unit.

Chapter 5

'This wasn't her home anymore,' he said. Those words penetrated her mind like a steel rod, blocking out all other thoughts. Her parents' and brothers' bodies weren't even in the ground and the land that had housed them, the land that sustained them, that sustained the empire, wasn't theirs any longer. It was already assigned to someone else. The new owners would take occupation within a month, or lose it themselves. That was the emperor's way. Replace and fill when gaps presented themselves. Focus on the living and not the dead. Why honor what could not hold onto life?

It was these thoughts that bounced around in her brain on the walk back to the farmhouse. The house that was no longer her home. Someone else would call it home. Someone on an imperial waiting list. A married couple who got bumped to the top because her family had been bumped off by rebels. It was these thoughts that rolled around on the back of her tongue as she packed her few positions into Oscar's cargo space. A doll that her sister had made for her when the one they shared tore. Her second dress, the one she wore to church and socials. It was buttery yellow and a little short in the ankles, but it was better than nothing. The quilt her mother had sewn for her. There was nothing else in the house that was hers. Everything else was shared. Everything else would become their property.

Even her mother's wedding ring would become property of the state. The price of cleanup and reassignment.

"Miss?" one of the cleanup crews asked as she came down the stairs. Miranda looked up at him. "We're all done. You need to get on the transport if you want a ride into town." It was less of a statement and more of an order. She couldn't stay here. If the new family were onworlders, then they could be here in less than a day. Ready to bring the rest of the harvest in and stop the fire from taking the house. Until then, the barn and animals would remain in suspended animation.

There was nothing for her here. Not even to hand the keys over. She took one last look at the house and her life, then she stepped into the transport van. It sped off as quick as the Ironsides had called it, taking her away from the only life she'd ever known.

"So when will we be arriving in town?" she asked. The back of the van consisted of two long benches filled to the brim with random equipment. Test tubes, laser guns, jugs of chemicals and other things that Miranda couldn't place. In between all of it sat two officers. To squeeze her in she had to move a black bag full of tools onto her lap. Otherwise she would have been standing.

The bag was heavy. The weight of it cut off the circulation to her legs. She imagined that the thing was filled with lead weights. The kind her brothers used to use when fishing. She knew the town was far in a hover cart, but as the light from the split window across the top of the van faded to black she was beginning to wonder how far it was really.

Neither of the men stirred. One snorted in his sleep. The other had a headset.

"I have to pee," she confessed. Unlike the soldiers, she wasn't outfitted with a depository extermination unit. Neither of the men responded. She would just have to hold it.

At some point the movement of the van must have lulled her to sleep because daylight streamed through the window. She rubbed her eyes.

"We're here," said the first soldier. The other one nodded and opened the door. The urge to pee was way too high. All she cared about was getting to a restroom as fast as her legs could carry her. She bolted from the van, leaving her untalkative travel companions in her dust.

In front of her was the largest building she'd ever seen. It rose into the sky, blotting out the sun. A tower of glass and metal shaped into a spiral, it gleamed like the diamond in her sister's wedding ring, only much much bigger.

She stopped on the steps and staired. She definitely wasn't in the lowlands anymore. They'd taken her all the way to the closest thing Oreilly 13 had to a capital. Her mother had talked about the ocean city before. 'Too many people,' she'd said. Too many buildings. Too much of everything. But not details like this. Miranda didn't know what to think. She closed her mouth and walked on. Her legs cramped up as she climbed the stairs to the entrance, but her bladder pushed her to the top. She wouldn't be the country bumpkin that peed all over the building stairs.

She forced herself to enter. It felt like being swallowed whole. This was a mechanical whale and she was but one of many victims it claimed. Inside she spotted a help desk.

"Please. Restroom," she asked the droid behind a screening desk. It was a large, ornate, carved stone and wood thing that jutted out at odd angles, cutting off people's views around it. He pointed a metal hand to the left. She hobbled down the hallway. Doors marked with different offices and names both of people and what they did inclosed her on every side. Then thankfully she saw the restroom. She shuffled in.

After relieving herself she made her way back to the main desk.

"Where would I find information about reassimilation?" she asked. The machine behind the desk looked up from his input projection. His nametag read Derik.

"Down the hall and to the right." Derik looked back down. Miranda squared her shoulders, turned on her heels, and headed back down the hall she'd just run down.

"You'll need an appointment," Derik shouted after her. She turned back to the desk.

"How do I get one of those?" she asked. He turned his projections around so she could read it.

"Type your name here," he pointed to a block on a form. Miranda entered her name. He turned the projection back around, typed in a few other things and then they waited.

"They will see you now."

Miranda sighed and turned back towards the hallway.

"Third door on the right," he said as an afterthought. She shot a smile back at him and walked back down the hallway for what she hoped was the last time.

Behind the third door on the right was a small waiting room. A large projection screen. The door clicked closed behind her, leaving no trace that it had ever been.

"Please put your hand on the pedestal," chimed a friendly female voice. Miranda looked around for the pedestal. A solid metal thing that came up to her waist appeared to rise up from the middle of the floor. Flat on top, it was circular in the way a cylinder is round on the sides, but flat on the bottom. Aside from the pedestal, there were three chairs each in a corner of the room, making a kind of semi circle out of the small space. They were white with tall backs and oversized cushions. Each one had the same throw pillow in the same light blue print. It sat center between the three chairs.

As she looked around she lost track of which way she'd come in. With no doors and no windows there was no way to remember. This scared some part of her, but she pushed it deep inside. Disappearing walls. Building stretching to the sky. People that sat at a desk and told you where to go. No wonder her mother didn't say much about this place. It was so removed from their simple life on the farm that it made talking about it hard.

"Please put your hand on the pedestal," the voice chimed again, breaking into her rising panic. Its friendly female tone hit her with sweet sugar on her ears. Miranda surmised that it must be a recording. No person could keep that cheerful a tone the second time they had to give instructions like 'put your hand on the pedestal'. Miranda moved to obey, then hesitated. She was unsure if following the instructions of a faceless sweet voice was the right thing to do.

"Please put your hand on the pedestal," it chimed again.

Oscar beeped by her side.

"Ok, ok, I'm putting my hand on the pedestal," she said. She placed her right palm straight down on the pedestal. There was a light glow emanating from the top. It circled her hand for what felt like minutes. Miranda tried to pull away, but her hand was stuck. 'Like flypaper,' she thought.

"Thank you," said the female voice. The lights stopped and Miranda got her hand back. There was nothing like this in her education classes. Maybe pedestals and doorless rooms were a capital thing that most farm girls like her would never be allowed to witness. She should consider herself fortunate and not scared out of her whits.

"Miranda Farmer. Daughter of Micah and Mary Farmer. M district of the colonial planet Oreilly 13. Please have a seat." Miranda glared at the chairs. If she followed the voice's instructions this time, would she remain trapped to the seat of her choice?

"Miranda Farmer. Daughter of Micah and Mary Farmer. M district of the colonial planet Oreilly 13. Please have a seat."

Miranda sat. Oscar stayed glued to her leg. She tried to stand and found that thankfully she could.

"Miranda Farmer. Daughter of Micah and Mary Farmer. M district of the colonial planet Oreilly 13. Please have a seat."

She sat again. The voice was boss, Miranda decided.

A pair of lights appeared on either side of the walls. They started at the top and moved down the walls until they disappeared at the bottom. The movement was slow at first. Then it started to gain speed. Miranda felt as if she was being pressed by a giant hand down into her chair. She gripped the arms of the chair, her nails digging in for dear life.

"Please God, save me!" she cried. Something went 'ding.' Everything stopped. The lights rested at the top of the room again, the pressure she'd been feeling instantly lifted. She took a breath she didn't know she'd been holding.

A part of the wall became a door and slid away to reveal another room.

"Miranda Farmer. Daughter of Micah and Mary Farmer. M district of the colonial planet Oreilly 13. Please exit. Thank you for choosing Riolu Transportation for your booking needs. Have a great day."

Miranda stood up and tried to walk towards the open door. Her legs wobbled underneath her. She felt like she was falling, even though she could see her legs and the ground on which they stood. It made her head ache.

On the other side of the door was a short hallway littered with brightly colored boxes with large holes in weird places. Miranda watched as people darted in and out of the holes carrying papers and other things with them. An android sat behind the desk closest to Miranda. It beckoned her over.

"Miranda Farmer. Daughter of Micah and Mary Farmer. M district of the colonial planet Oreilly 13. You have been checked in," it said in the same sickly sweet voice that had come out of the walls in the last room.

"Sure," Miranda said. She didn't know what they'd check, or how she could be outside without leaving the building. But it didn't matter. After what she'd just gone through she didn't feel like questioning what was happening now.

A man in a gray and yellow suit walked out of a purple box straight past Miranda and the droid with an oversized holo pad in his hands. He stopped right past them, then turned back to them. The man had a kind face, older, but nice. He reminded her of her father with this receding hairline and laugh lines around his eyes. She stopped to look at him.

"Miranda Farmer," he said.

"Yes," Miranda answered out of habit.

"Ryan Protocol," the man said. He reached out his hand. He shook her hand, his fingers smooth and clammy in her rough tan ones. "Come this way, Ms. Farmer." He headed back into the purple room. Miranda followed. The room was even tinier than the one with the three chairs. It held a desk and two chairs. The chairs and desk nearly touched. Miranda couldn't help but think that everything in the room from the bright purple walls to the cramped furniture was too big and too small at the same time.

"Please have a sweet." He took the lid off the candy bowl on his desk and offered it out to her. Inside was a rainbow of different colored sweets, each individually wrapped and ready to be sucked on.

She picked a red one hoping for pinkberry, but wasn't too disappointed when it turned out to be april blossom.

"So, Ms. Farmer," he started. "We have a bit of a problem." She sucked on the sweet and listened. "You are seventeen and an orphan. Normally when a tragedy like yours occurs you would be relocated to your nearest family, or with a family that can use your skill set. Unfortunately, farmers are not a needed commodity. Nor do you, as a female, maintain any needed skills that are."

He paused for breath. Miranda sucked harder on the candy. So cooking and cleaning and bread making and fire starting weren't needed skills to this man in his box. The flavor of april blossom melted down to pure sugar on her tongue.

"You are also not old enough for marriage. Even if we awarded you to the state, which is not a likely scenario since you have a living sister still, yes?" He looked up from his paperwork and leveled his gaze on her. It wasn't a harsh stare. More of a father to a problem child stare. Miranda nodded her head. He made a hand motion at her. As if she needed to say it aloud. Make it real.

"Yes," she said, "Mary Farmer."

"Hmm," I see that she has been relocated to..." he stopped talking and scrolled through his paperwork, "a new terraform in the Galdec sector." He took off his glasses and rubbed the bridge of his nose.

"That is problematic."

"Problematic," Miranda repeated. She felt like a pet parrot. So what if her sister had found a man? So what if the two of them had left world? Her new husband was a third son, never going to inherit, and Mary was a daughter. They were both farm raised. It made sense for the two of them to jump on the Relocationary Act of 3546. Most of Miranda's friends were planning to do just that. First you had to find a willing partner.

"Yes, problematic." He set his holo stack down and leaned back into his chair. "You see. Being that she is your closest family, she would be the ideal choice for guardianship. Sadly, her exact planet record is sealed. Even if we could send you, we wouldn't know which exact planet to send you to. You have no other male relations within this system. No aunts or uncles on either side on the planet."

"Or grandparents," Miranda added. She was trying to be helpful.

"Or grandparents," he agreed. "Both your father's siblings are across the galaxy on other colonies and your mother was an only child. Her parents died in a raid before she was married." He was not telling her anything she didn't already know. Her family had been large because her parents chose to have multiple kids. It had never bothered her up until this moment that that was all the family she had.

"Legally we cannot send you offworld to anyone not of direct blood relation," he continued. Miranda rolled what was left of the sweet across her tongue. The was developing an edge and would cut her if she wasn't careful.

"In cases like this, you would become a ward of Oreilly 13, but you are too old. Wards have to be younger than sixteen years of age at the time of wardship. One year is not long enough to assign and place you. Since we have to give at least six months to your family to reach out and claim you, and so on."

"So the question is, what to do with you?" he stated.

The words felt like a smack to her backside. Bad little orphan. It's all your fault your whole family was killed by rebels and you became the state's problem.

"What are my options?" Miranda asked. He'd just spent fifteen minutes outlining what she couldn't do. He could at least be helpful and tell her what she could do.

"Well, we could issue you an emancipation statement. It would legally allow you the status of adulthood, for the purposes of employment and housing and such. But an emancipation statement doesn't deter the fact that marriage is the only option for a farmer to stay in their profession. You would have to be put into a different work sector, but which one?"

Miranda kept still. She did not want to distract him. He was giving her valuable information and she wanted that to continue. He looked her over from head to toe evaluating her value.

"You're not a pushover. Are you a strong girl?" he asked.

"I can lift a bag of flour and carry it across the barn," she said, thinking about heavy lifting exercises she'd done throughout the year. He scowled.

"And I can pick a bushel of monk fruit in an hour," she added. It wasn't really a sign of strength, but a bushel of monk fruit was a lot of heavy lifting over a long period of time, having to carry the bucket and all. He shook his head.

"Fine, fine. It is probably for the best," he said. There was a long pause where he faced her strait on, looked her in the eyes, and sighed. "How do you feel about joining the military?

Chapter 6

Miranda stared at him, eyes wide. Her mouth moved to open. No words came to mind so she shut it closed. She opened it again, determined to answer the question.

"I guess I never have." The words poured out of her.

"Wonderful!" he said. Ryan turned around in his swivel chair and pressed a couple of buttons on the wall. A panel slid open. He reached inside and pulled out a camouflage hat.

He put it on his head and swiveled back around to face her. Nothing else seemed to change. His face was more somber, if that was possible. He took back the candy bowl and replaced it with grapes. His smile was still sly. His badge now read Ryan Recruiter.

Miranda blinked. Had changing into a hat changed his name? The evidence was staring her in the face. Miranda sat there as Ryan now Recruiter typed furiously away at his vid screen.

"Well, it looks like everything is in order here. Just gotta hit this Signature button." He turned the vid screen towards her. She made her mark on the line he indicated.

"There, almost done." He pressed a button on the screen.

"Most Basic pickups happen every Tuesday. Today's Monday, so that would be tomorrow morning at 0845. Be at Launch Pad

Bravo, Bay 6 for the Gagarin System." Turning back to his computer, he said, "Mysti, get our new recruit a uniform."

Something in the office went 'ding.' A piece of the wall opened up and a drawer presented itself.

Miranda was afraid to put her hands in the drawer. It might decide at that moment to slide back close taking her hands with it.

"It's ok," Ryan assured her.

"Please pick up your request," said the helpful female voice.

'That must be Mysti,' Miranda thought as she reached in and picked up the clothes.

"Thank you," said the voice as the drawer closed with a click. The wall looked unbroken. Miranda traced it with a finger. She felt no edge. Not even a break in the surface. She shivered.

"Beep beep," Oscar said from her side. After all this time she'd forgotten that he was still there.

"Oh, Oscar. Oscar!" she said.

"I forgot to ask," Miranda said as she balanced all of her new gear on her lap. The pile consisted of a pair of boots stacked on top of a green pair of pants, with a shirt and vest tucked underneath them. A pair of black socks stuck out of the boots, which kept wanting to slide off the top of the pile. "Is it ok to bring my droid along? I mean, can new recruits have droids?" Miranda reached out to Oscar and pushed a series of buttons. Out popped his transit drawer. It was one of the few things she'd grabbed in her mad dash from the house. Her best dress, some undergarments, and the locket her mother had given her when she was twelve. She stuck the whole pile on top of everything else and hit the close button.

"Technically, you can bring one carry on from home. If the carry on itself is the droid then it would be allowed," Ryan said, adjusting his vid screen. "But mostly they're not something we get very often."

He barely paused before saying, "That's an interesting request for a new recruit. Do you have a droid in mind?" Oscar rolled out from under her skirt and beeped at him.

"This droid, Sir," Miranda replied.

"Beep beep beep beep beeeeeep," Oscar said indignantly.

"He's wondering why you haven't noticed him before," she said.

Ryan scratched the top of his head.

"My apologies," he said, but you could tell he didn't really mean it.

"Beep beep be," Oscar replied. Miranda stiffed a giggle.

"What did he say?" Ryan asked.

"Can't you understand droid?" Miranda asked. All the members of her family could understand Oscar to some extent or another. Even if only she and mother could translate every word, her brothers always got the jist of what the droid communicated.

Ryan shook his head.

"He says, 'Your apology is accepted,'" she answered, covering for what the droid had really said. Ryan could have Oscar taken away from her and she didn't want that. The man's nice demeanor could be hiding all kinds of cruelty. She did not want to get on his bad side any more than she already was.

"Beeeep," said the little droid. Miranda crossed her arms and looked at him. 'Don't press your luck,' she mouthed.

"Interesting," Ryan said. "I need to mark that in your file."

Miranda sighed. She felt like a damsel in distress being saved by her father. Only this man was nothing like her father, so maybe more of an eccentric uncle who she never wanted around. And that was not how she wanted to feel. She wanted to feel powerful, in control, happy even. But she didn't know, without her family, if that was possible. She took two big breaths and popped another grape into her mouth.

Miranda stayed in Mr. Ryan's office for another hour filling out paperwork and setting up her emancipation records. Every time she opened her mouth to say something he would shove the grape bowl under her nose. She would eat one and her mouth would remain full while he filled in another form for her. Miranda had never had this much fruit in her life.

At the end of the hour he pressed a button on his holo pad, filing away all the extra documentation.

"You are free to go, Ms. Farmer," he said shaking her hand one last time. She shook it back, not wanting to be rude, but not really understanding.

"Free to go where?" she asked. She was afraid of the answer being 'nowhere.' That there was no place in this world for her.

"The transport station is three blocks down on the right. Can't miss it. Big banners of Ironsides up and down the building. Good day." With those words he escorted her back the way she'd come; past the droid, back into the room with three chairs, saw her safely to one of the seats, and then stepped back out of the room.

Chapter 7

Before she knew it she was standing back outside in front of the building, staring up at its grandeur.

The sun was high in the sky. While the visit had taken only a few hours, to Miranda it had felt like days. But that was the nature of grand places. They stole your breath and your time, whether you wanted them to or not.

"He'd said that it was down the street on the left?" Miranda asked Oscar. The little droid had stayed safely tucked up under her skirt the entire time she'd been in the office. Now he was venturing out, if only to see the street.

"Beep beep boop," Oscar said.

"You didn't hear him?" Miranda repeated.

"Beeeep," Oscar.

"Much help you are," she said. She turned left and headed down the street. Nothing was as grand as the main city tower. The glass structure loomed miles above even the tallest of the town's other buildings. More sported two, many three stories. Their fronts were made to draw people into the shops. Food stalls, tailor shops, tech stores lined the street on either side. Large glass windows marked with the names of the business and what they did in gold and silver lettering. Pretty covers shaded potential customers from the rain or, on a day like today, the hot sun.

This one had a brick facade. That one wood. Still another chipped stone. It was all overwhelming and beautiful in a melting pot kind of way.

Miranda's chest swelled with pride. Two generations ago this planet was uninhabitable waste of space rock. Now it was a thriving cog in the imperial wheel. The edge that kept the dark of space at bay. She was a part of that. Her family was a part of that. Her grandfather an original settler. Then might had their lives cut short. But the sacrifice was not in vain.

The street appeared to stretch on forever.

"You know, Oscar," Miranda said, "I think we've gone too far." The street had turned from merchant stalls to residential. "The transport office wouldn't be here. We need to turn back."

"Lost, little lamb?" called a voice from a nearby alley. Miranda watched as a man in a long black coat melted out of the alley's shadow into existence on the pavement before her.

She backed up slowly, her face smiling.

"No, not lost," she told him. She was so focused on smiling and walking backwards to get away from the oil man that she didn't notice the giant until she ran right into him.

"Oh, I think you are," said the man, the curve in his smile deepening. She turned to run and found a wall of flesh in front of her.

"Very lost indeed."

That was the last thing she heard before a giant's fist came down on her head and the world turned black.

She awoke to a stream of light hitting her eyes in a strange diamond pattern. Flashes against the back of her eyelids, then darkness, then more flashes. Something jostled her. She bumped her head into something as she tried to right herself. It felt hard, but not brick hard. More like wood.

Her hands were tied behind her back, making it hard to move. Even worse, she realized why the world looked like diamonds of light to her spinning head. Someone had put a burlap sack over her face and secured it with a rope at her neck. The fabric chafed. She would have a burn mark when they took the thing off. If they took the thing off.

"Oscar," she whispered. "Oscar." If her droid was still with her, then she'd be able to get herself out for this, but without him... She didn't want to think about it. She'd heard horror stories about girls going missing off town streets all throughout the galaxy. There were plenty of reasons to snatch a girl. All of them boiled down to brides. A man that couldn't find a willing bride might pay for one on the black market so he could get his homestead.

If you were pretty enough they might drug you and sell you to a Creshi, but that was rare. Powerful men had no problem paying for second and third wives, or husbands. A small planet like Orielly 13 wouldn't attract that kind of clientele. So most likely Miranda was headed to a marriage market.

If her father and brothers were here this would never have happened. There were laws against it. But here she was alone, no droid, and no way out.

Big hands picked her up from the cart and set her up on a platform of some kind.

A crowd roared in the distance. Even from beneath the mask she could hear them. This was no private auction they'd taken her to. This was a large affair, with at least a hundred or more men in need of a wife to claim their homestead. The smell of rotting hay and animal waste hit her nose. The burlap bag did little to hold back the stench. Barn. They had hijacked a barn. Probably a one-time use. Close enough out of the city to draw a crowd, but not far enough away to warrant a recurring visit. Smugglers couldn't be choosers, she guessed.

"Well," she told herself as she waited for her turn at the block. "It could be worse. You could be going to your death." The crowd roared again. She could hear it now. The deep canter of an auctioneer's voice. It was so fast it blended in with the flashing light and the overwhelming animal stink.

"Great day for a wedding," she told her captor. His big hands pushed her forward. She was going to live through this. She was going to live, she told herself.

Men might buy brides, but they knew better than to kill them. You lost your homestead if you lost your wife. Even if you had kids. Homesteads were held in both names. Even though it couldn't be passed to a girl child, it would revert back to government land if your wife died before you had a married son.

Even if you got remarried, you'd lose all the work you put into the place. You'd have to start new with a new homestead. Years of work lost.

"It won't be too bad of a life," she told herself. "You're a farm girl, after all." Death of a spouse meant loss of your homestead. That's why the marriage age of eighteen was so strict. Having a kid before eighteen greatly reduced your chance of living. It was the one thing all the Creshy doctors couldn't cure. Too many risks, when all they had to do was limit marriage to eighteen plus, and the problems solved themselves.

Blackmarket places like this didn't care about age. They'd fake all the paperwork so the age limit wasn't a problem. Even an irate customer with a dead wife on their hands couldn't find the sellers to complain to. And once settled on the planet, there was no coming back. Transport lines took years to develop, a new terraformed world could collect tax for ten years before the first trading vessel touched base in the system, and only after at least three planets had been terraformed was it even worth the fuel.

There was no one to catch you in the lie. No one to track missing daughters if they got you offworld. No one to save her. The loneliness of Miranda's circumstance hit her hard. For the first time, the death of her family felt real. Tears welled up behind her eyes and spilled out. Large crying sobs racked her body. As she stood there bound, dirty, and about to be sold to the highest bidder, she let all the fear and sadness and loss go.

Her captor gave her a shake.

"Brighten up, lovely," he said in an accent she couldn't place, "your turn here in a bit."

Miranda didn't care. She let her body wash her emotions clean until she'd rung herself dry.

"Right then, your turn." He thrust her forward with one hand and pulled the hood of with the other.

Part of her wished she could see herself. Dirty, covered in mud and blood and soot. Her clothes a wrinkled mess from falling and climbing and being kidnapped. Her eyes bloodshot from crying. Her hair at odd angles from the hood. She must look an absolute fright. It would limit the men that would bid on her. That was ok. She'd be sold. She was sure of that, but she might get a nice man. A too nice man without much money, but too quiet or shy to get a girl.

The auctioneer started the bid at a middle ground price, then proceeded to talk so fast Miranda couldn't keep up. No one took it. The auctioneer dropped the price. Still no takers. He dropped the price again. Not a single person coughed, raised a hand, nothing. Stopping in his incessant calling for a moment the auctioneer said, "This one might look a little rough and tumble, but that might mean she's even better in the sheets." He winked at the audience members and went back to his calling. One hand near the far back tentatively went in the air.

The auctioneer grabbed onto it like a lifeline. He put only the minimal effort into trying to start a bid.

"Pretty little mud pie going once. Pretty little mud pie going twice." On the word 'twice' the back door of the barn blew off its hinges, showering the people closest to it in splinters. MIlitary guards poured through the doors in their stark white uniforms.

"This is an official government raid. Remain where you are," said an Ironside. Miranda recognised the voice. At their center of the flood stood an Ironside with a slightly dented helmet. For the second time in her life Miranda was relieved to see the best of the empire's soldiers coming to her rescue.

Someone from the audience fired a blaster at the door. Everyone scattered. The women on the platform screamed. Chained as they were to one another, all they could do was duck for cover. Miranda lay exposed as blasters fired in every direction.

"Get down," someone screamed at her. MIranda stood there, watching the red and yellow lights flash around her in every direction. She felt the sting of a blast bolt singe her hair.

Oscar beeped a warning at her, but Miranda was too dazed to respond. The droid rolled straight into her knees, knocking them out from under her. She landed with a thud face first into the boards of the makeshift stage they'd constructed in the barn just as a faser blast scarred where she'd been standing. Her arms failed to come up in time. Her nose hit the boards with a sickening crunch. Blood gushed down her face.

That woke her up. She curled herself into a ball, afraid to move, gun fire going off around her in every direction. Even when it stopped she still heard it ringing in her ears. The 'pew pew's echoed around her head.

"Are you ok?" said that familiar voice. A hand touched her back, turning her over. She looked up into the mask of the Ironside, his gear fluctuating between camo mode and silver visibility. Miranda laughed. He looked too much like a ghost for her comfort.

"They got away," a soldier reported to the Ironside. His name tag read Axel. Odd for a last name. Maybe they went by first names in the imperial forces.

"Here, let me help you up." The Ironside gave her his hand. She used it to gain her balance.

"Do we have a key for these?" the Ironside asked, looking to his left and right. He looked right at the soldier Axel. Axel shrugged. The Ironside held the chains in one hand and pulled a blaster from his left side with the other. Miranda pulled back, cringing at the weapon, but the Ironside held fast.

"Pew pew," the gun went off. The chains fell away, melted to slag by the power of a close range shot.

Miranda stood there no longer in chains, rubbing her wrists, thankful that the hood was no longer on and that the second most frightening thing that had ever happened in her life was now behind her. She wiped the blood from her nose with a corner of her dress that looked clean enough.

IMPERIAL EDGE

It was a simple matter, getting saved. Ironsides breaking up an illegal auction was probably something they did on planetoids every day.

But to her it was like magic. Something out of a fairy tale. The knight coming to the princess' rescue; things that she only read about in offworld stories. From the original age of imperialism, back before the Empire was a solidified form with all of the different planets being terraformed by the First Ones. It was more romantic than her poor little head could handle at this moment. She sat there contemplating all of this, caught up in her own daydreams, until she had heard the words.

The Ironside swore. He stomped down one booted foot, and then the other, oblivious to the way that it shook the stage that the girls sat on.

Miranda was one of only 16 that escaped the auction. The fleeing buyers had taken their brides with them if they'd already bought.

She could have sworn there had been hundreds gathered, or at least one hundred gathered. Better not to exaggerate such things.

"I could have sworn that they were going to be here," the Ironside said.

"Yes, sir," said the other Ironside, saluting him.

"We caught this one trying to escape with the cash box." The soldier, whose name tag said Cash, pushed a man towards the first Ironside.

"Bring him here," said the Ironside. Miranda made a mental note to try and learn his name. She'd thought that he'd be in her life just that once. But know she wasn't so sure. Nothing seemed sure anymore.

"Yes, sir," said Cash. They pulled forward a raggedy looking man, his teeth barely there. Who knows where he had lost them; either to rot, or to fights. His hair was struggling to cover a bald spot. His shoulders looked strong from years of labor. His hands were hardened with calluses, his clothes nondescript farmers garb; blue jeans, and a light white shirt. Nothing about him stood out from anyone else that had been on the grounds, except for his sneer. Under his curved lip was the kind of man that could never be broken. Even when slapped and beaten and put on a pole for display that sardonic sneer would cut through the mind of any that tried to break this man.

"Who tipped you off?" the Ironside said. His dented helmet made his voice crackle. The man spat on the floor but kept his mouth shut. His eyes burned with hate as he looked at the Ironside. The Ironside tipped his head towards the soldiers holding the ringleader. The one that had brought him over punched him in the gut.

The man bent over in serious pain. But when he lifted his head, his eyes showed that shrewd intelligence.

"Who tipped you off?" the Ironside asked again. Another punch to the gut.

"No one," he said, spitting blood this time.

"Well if no one tipped you off, then how did the rebels get away." It was not a question, but the man answered it anyway.

"What rebels? I know of no rebels. I am just a businessman," he said. His smirk tugged at the corner of his bleeding mouth.

"Fine. What was your business here?"

The man shrugged, as much as a man being held by two armed soldiers could shrug.

"I'm just a tradesman." He waved his hands to the left and right. His arms, trapped between the soldiers, remained unmoving.

"And what are you trading? Wives?" the Ironside stated.

"Yes," the businessman said. That's what Miranda was going to call him from now on. She refused to give such trash a real name. It didn't matter if she would ever see him again. In her mind he would always be a businessman.

"Your legal paperwork for these poor girls," the Ironside reached forward as if expecting the trapped man to produce the video cards on the spot.

"My compadres have it stacked in the back," he said, his smile unmoved. "Besides, what would rebels want with girls? What rebel would want a wife; so he could settle down in the far reaches of the Empire? Away from the action and target of the capital?"

Cash looked at the Ironside. "We're not going to get anything out of him." He punched the business man again for good measure; once in the stomach, and once in the head.

The man coughed blood. The soldier went for a third punch. The Ironside stopped his arm mid swing and stepped in, his mask against the face of the man.

"They were here for something" said the Ironside. "And one way or another, you are going to tell me what they where here for."

The Ironside tipped his head to the left. The two soldiers dragged the man away. He would be interrogated later in a much more civilized setting. But for the moment the girls had to be dealt with. He shooed the third soldier away with his hand.

"You girls are free to go," he said to the girls that were still huddled against the stage. They began to relax slightly, thankful that they were not going to be pieced off to some colonial place with a husband that had bought them instead of loved them enough to try their hand. A man undeserving of their talents. The Ironside probably thought so little them. Girls easily caught up in the schemes of money grabbing men.

Miranda wasn't the ugliest among those that were gathered, but she certainly did not look worthy in her stained work dress. All covered in dirt and blood and mud caked on; such was the price of the days that she had been having. Now she could add blaster dust and wood chips.

Then she heard it. Oscar's voice in the distance.

"Beep beep," he said. She looked up to see him rolling up next to the Ironside. The Ironside looked down at the little droid and gave him a pat on the head.

"Beep" said Oscar, rolling up the stage. He tried hiding under her skirts. Not that there was much to hide.

"Thank you, Oscar," Miranda said. "It's so good to see you." She gave the little droid a hug. He'd saved her life; the least she owed him was a hug.

The little droid—the only thing left from her old life. It didn't hurt that he had all of her clothing packed away somewhere in one of his drawers. It just meant so much to her to have a piece of home. A piece of reality not tied to everything that had happened in the last few days. If she had had the tears to cry, they would have been streaming down her face. But she was all dried up.

Her lips cracked. Her nose a fountain of dried blood. Her eyes were swollen from hours and hours of crying. There was no moisture left for tears of joy.

Chapter 8

She wasn't as far away from the shining ocean city as she'd feared. The hood had definitely caused her more confusion, because it had felt like they traveled for days. All that time between blacking out and waking had been minutes, not days or weeks. She was still trapped in the nightmare of this day.

When she stepped out of the barn, she could see the outline of the central tower on the horizon; its glass surface a diamond reflecting the sun and sea. They were in one of the upscale farms that bordered the city. Not more than an hour or two hover-ride away.

Her mother had told her about these farms. They were gifts from the emperor to soldiers that fought in the Galactic Wars. Unlike a homestead grant, these were endowed to the family indefinitely. If the descendants didn't want to live there, they could rent them out and receive a portion of the crops produced. It was the best real estate on the planet. Sometimes when families were between renters they fell prey to illicit actions, like bride auctions. But they never stayed empty for long. The protection of the greater city and the richness of the land made being a renter worth it.

"Are you okay, miss?" asked the Ironside. It was an honest question. One that she was not likely to get from any of the other soldiers.

She looked up at the Ironside, noticing the line of his shoulders. How much broader he looked than any of her brothers. He was tall, too. Much taller than her father. Did he remember her? She didn't think so. But it was so hard to read concern through a mechanically filtered voice. He was a hard-light hologram underneath that helmet, for all she knew. She couldn't even see his eyes. There was no way of knowing what he saw when he looked upon her.

Was he still after the rebels that had murdered her family? She had the answer to the second question, even if she'd never know the reality of the first. Yes. He was. She didn't need to ask. He'd said as much as he interviewed the business man. Even in her mind, the words crawled with sarcasm.

"Miss?" the Ironside asked again. Had she been so lost in her own thoughts that she failed to answer him?

'He must think I'm a halfwit,' she thought.

"No, I am not alright." The truth slipped from her mouth before she could stop it.

"Not alright," he repeated back at her. It was funny. He most likely expected her to state platitudes, but after the day—or maybe it was days now, she didn't know—she'd had, nice wasn't in her.

"Yes. I am very much not alright," she stated again. He must not have been used to people telling him unfiltered truth, because he simply stared at her.

'If only I could see his face,' she thought. 'I bet his mouth would be open.' But she couldn't tell through the helmet.

"The droid yours?" asked the Ironside.

"What's your name?" Miranda asked, ignoring his question. He'd made to change the subject, so if they were changing the subject then she wanted to know some things about her two-time rescuer in the off-chance that he'd rescue her again.

"What?" he stuttered.

"What is your name?" she said again, making sure to pronounce everything without slurring any of the words, but not slowing down as if talking to a child. He was no child, this man in uniform. She was going to find his name out, but it didn't hurt to be direct.

"Eric," he said. "Pr... well, just Eric."

"Do they strip you of your last name when you enter the army?" she asked. She was thinking about whether they would call her 'Farmer' in basic, or if she would become Miranda. Free from her old life.

"No," he said standing a little straighter.

"No?" she repeated. This conversation was going nowhere. "What kind of a man doesn't have a last name?"

"The kind that lived on a planet that didn't give em." He slurred the last word. Miranda stifled a giggle. So she was pushing on a button. She looked down at his gun and swallowed hard.

Maybe it wasn't good to aggravate the highly trained killer with a laser gun that could blow her to pieces with a single shot.

She stood on wobbly knees. They shifted under her, refusing to take her weight just long enough to throw off her center of balance. He caught her in his arms before she took him down with her.

"Thanks," she said, grateful to be steady.

"You are welcome," he replied. He was so polite, she almost thought that he was well bred. But that was the problem with thinking. No well bred Creshi would be caught dead out on a terraform planet like Oreilly 13. Even if they were chasing down killer rebels. Nobles weren't allowed to endanger themselves like that. They were too valuable to the empire.

"Can I help in any way?" he asked, taking a step back from her. He probably wanted distance, given that she could easily collapse again. He didn't want a girl to take him down for a second time in front of his men.

"Yes, I need to go to the transportation office," she said.

"The transportation office," he repeated. Was he a patriot? Miranda began to wonder. He kept repeating everything she said. It felt like the whole conversation was a repeat.

"Yes. You sent me to the main offices, I joined the military and they told me to go to the transportation center. So I can catch the next transport to basic," she said.

She waited. He stood there still as a rock. Seconds ticked away in her mind. She shifted from one foot to the other and back again, waiting. Her mind had no room to wonder. She was fried. Filled to the brim with everything that was going on in her life.

"I can do that," he said. Eric said. She was going to start calling him Eric. Not Ironside. Not him, but Eric.

"Great," she replied. She looked around the room. Some of the girls were still giving statements. Others were wrapped in blankets. All of them were being treated by soldiers with snakes on their bags. Miranda had never seen a snake in real life. The creatures were rare. Kept in special cages. Bread as pets for high ranking Creshi. They never left Cresh. One of the most dangerous animals. They once escaped into the wilds of a newly terraformed planet before the Empire was formed. They killed all of the human inhabitants within a year. The planet had to be reterraformed. Even then, it was abandoned. Left to rot. The stuff of night campfire stories.

They looked like S's with heads. That's how the stories described them, and that's what Miranda was seeing on their bags.

It was one thing to see things on a holopad. The 3D projections could look quite real. But they weren't; there was a level of fake to them. Everyone knew that they were just light reflecting off the world. But it was another thing to see it in person. A real medic bag.

Miranda stared in wonder, shook her head, and then moved on. The Ironside had already started. Eric. Eric had already started marching off towards a transport unit.

"Soldier," he said.

"Yes, sir," said the plain clothes soldier, saluting the Ironside; Eric brushed the salute away.

"Commandeer me a transport unit." He threw a look over shoulder towards Miranda. She stood there, droid in arm, smiling.

They were finally doing it. They were finally going someplace.

"Yes, sir!" said the soldier. He ran off to get a hovercraft.

Eric turned back to Miranda. "That will suit, yes?" The words came out stagnant, as if he was not used to asking for others' opinions. Instead he was more used to giving orders and having them followed.

'I must be quite a conundrum for you,' Miranda thought. A smirk formed on her lips. She soon wiped it off and put a blank smile on.

"Yes, that will be much appreciated," she said. It wasn't long before the soldiers came back with a hover vehicle. Eric dropped into the driver's seat and motioned Miranda to sit on the side passenger side.

It was an open vehicle, bars across the top, with four bucket seats. Short, stout, but a high-range hover that looked like it could go upwards to 30 or even 40 feet.

Not a standard five-to-eight foot hovercraft. The vehicle was military grade, of course, and painted in the desert colors that would blend in with both the forest and the wheat fields; an odd match of colors that made your eyes want to look away, and not stare directly at it. Camo paint was quite the thing, Miranda thought, a scary kind of thing.

Using the bar she hopped into the other side and kept hold of Oscar as she slid into the seat. The two of them jetted off, headed back towards the city and the recruitment office.

Flashes of fields blended into outer city houses and then into inner-city apartment buildings and flashy town homes of the rich. They weren't far out of town at all. In fact, she wondered why they'd gone as far as they did, and why she had thought that it was farther. Her mind felt jumbled, everything in pieces, her eyes swollen from crying.

Once they hit the edge of town she expected them to slow. For him to stop and let her out. When he didn't, when the town came and went, fear started to creep up into her veins.

"My stop was back there," she told him. He said nothing. If anything, he sped up. The world blurred past them.

"I appreciate the ride, but I needed to get on a transport unit to basic. That was back there," she continued. His head didn't even turn her way. Fields turned to tops of trees. They were climbing, headed into the mountains. They were going so fast all she could see was the shift from brown to green.

"You still have your droid?" Eric asked.

"Yes," Miranda said, trying to get back to the question at hand. "I can make sure that I'm ok until morning. I'll make the transport. Promise." She couldn't think of any other reason why he would be interested in her.

"Good." He increased his speed as he reached the edge of town. The countryside was blurring by. A strong wind whipped at her hair. She was glad it was secure behind her.

"I don't understand," Miranda confessed. The wind was turning sharp. Cold nipped at her dry lips, the cracks stinging as she pressed them together.

"Recruit Miranda Farmer, I am commandeering your active service to the Empire and the Crown." Miranda's mouth made a big O, but nothing came out.

"As a private you are now under my command. Do what you are told. Talk only when you are spoken to. Follow my lead," Eric said. Miranda shut her mouth with a click. After everything that she'd been through, she never thought that an Ironside would kidnap her in the name of the Emperor. This was turning out to be some adventure Oscar had gotten them into.

Chapter 9

"I'll deliver you to basic myself. When this is all over," Eric told her. She didn't doubt him. Didn't have a reason to. But what all this was, was yet to be seen. The possibilities played in Miranda's head over and over again until she made herself sick. The cold beat at her arms and legs.

Her blood soaked dress gave little protection against the change in weather. As they climbed higher into the mountain range, she worried herself until she had no more worries left in her. Eric noticed her shifting, shivering, and hit a button on the control panel. A stream of warm air poured out of the vent ducts, bathing her in a blanket of heat and numbing the day's happenings. It didn't take long for Miranda to fall asleep. The blur of her world passing by, the white nose of the wind whooping past her ears, the hum of the hover engine, the rays of summer sun; all pulled at her until she gave in yet again to her exhaustion.

She was caught off guard when the hovercraft came to an abrupt halt. Eric jumped out and headed towards what looks like a cave entrance in the side of a mountain. They were far away now, miles from any point of reference. No, she couldn't even see the farm valleys below. Or the tall shining tower of a city she had just once lifted her eyes to. But they were still on the planet; that much was certain. The hovercraft had incredible capabilities, but not interplanetary travel. That was at least something.

"I guess that means we're going here," she said to his back. She was slower to climb out of the hovercraft. Sleep was hard to shake when she needed it. She didn't know how long she had been asleep. The sun was still in the sky, so it could have been minutes or hours. Or it could have been the next day, as tired as she was. The next day was quite probable. She had no way to tell. The only person that could provide her with answers was walking away into a deep dark cave.

"Beep beep!" Oscar called from inside the hovercraft.

"I'm working on it," she told him as she helped him down from the craft. She sat him on the ground and made her way towards the cave, sure that he would follow. Oscar's love for everything dark and spooky was a well known factor in his adventures. One time when her sister was in charge of tracking down Oscar, Mary found him in a burl hole. He had chased a timbar down the hole, cornering the creature in its own borough, and kept it trapped until he was found.

Miranda felt safe putting him down, knowing that he would definitely follow. She walked past the mouth of the cave, assured that someone would probably do something with the hovercraft. Miranda took one last look back at the craft.

If this truly was a military base, then the Imperial forces would find something to do with their craft. Otherwise, why park it here? The Ironside wasn't stupid.

As she walked past the mouth of the cave, the sudden shift from light to darkness left her feeling cold and alone. She really wished they would get to a point where she could change out of her bloody dress. The last remnant of the life that she knew now clung to her, but only as a reminder of everything that she has lost and nothing of her future.

Ahead 10 feet stood a guardhouse. They had painted the exterior red-orange to match the color of the walls, so all anyone could see were the green bars sticking out, blocking the way further in.

"Halt!"

She heard the sound of a blaster rifle clicking back into charge mode. Miranda stopped. She couldn't see where the shot might come from, but she didn't want to press her luck.

"State your name, rank and business here," said a soldier who had suddenly appeared from apparently nowhere.

"Miranda Farmer. Private. I was told by the Ironside that went in before me to follow."

Sweat trickled down Miranda's neck. She'd never had a gun pointed at her before. Guns were wholly for hunting wild ors, or other creatures. Not to be ever pointed at people.

The soldier steadied the rifle in his hands. Miranda's legs twitched, wanting to run. There was a first time for everything. And apparently this was her first time to have a gun trained on her. And quite possibly the last.

Miranda waited. She hoped she had answered the question right, given the alternative of being shot. A long pause stretched out.

If one could hear clicking on a fazer rifle, Miranda's ears strained to do just that. The pause gave her eyes time to wander. The cave seemed to be lit from the inside, with sconces every three feet or so. Large metal cages held electric light from some unknown crystal; probably some expensive thing provided by the Empire for places like this: holes in the wall, where the military oversaw the edge outposts to protect the people on the planet.

Not that it helped protect her family from the rebels. Miranda clenched her fists tight. She wouldn't be running. Those rebels needed to pay. And if the Empire couldn't protect its own people, then she would become part of the force that protected the outer edge.

"You're free to pass," said the guard.

The green stick rose up to align with the guardhouse, melting into the wall as if both had never existed. Miranda gave a half salute, half wave at the guard and continued down the passageway. 20 feet in front of her It opened up into a large cavern that looked like some kind of landing bay. Different shuttle craft and fighter planes littered long stretches of carved stone that emptied out into the side of the mountain. There looked to be a place to land carriers and light shuttlecraft.

'Wow, that looks really interesting,' Miranda thought. Each of the crafts were made from a shiny, antioxidizing alloy. It was a special kind of mineral found only on certain planetoids in the deeper reaches of the star system. This metal had a high-impact grade resistance that could deflect asteroids and other debris that floated around in the depths of space that sometimes came into contact with orbiting ships. It was also extremely conductive.

And it was on that basis that interstellar ships could gather enough photon energy to reach hyperspace. Every second level Empire student knew that. But Miranda had never seen one in person, let alone a hangar full of them. Looking around, she noticed that it wasn't a single vehicle here; that was simply a planetary ship. All of them had interspace capable engines, and advanced AI droids that accompanied them.

Men and women ran around in different directions. Some to the left, some to the right, some carrying large stacks of tools. Others carried cans and food supplies, still more supplies for refueling. It all was one big mess of humanity before her eyes.

Docking fighter pilots in space suits, their helmets held under their arms as they walked and talked; men and women of all different planetary backgrounds; she had never seen such an array of human life gathered in one place before. Someone pushed her from behind. She stumbled forward into the path of an inbound jet when fingers grabbed her arm, pulling her to the side and out of the way of the planes wing.

"Thanks," Miranda said, "I'd be a pancake." She looked up to see the face of her rescuer, only to find it was Eric. She shook her head, startled out of her daze.

"This way," said Eric, ignoring her obvious stares. He looked good, too good without his helmet on: his hair, the cut of his jaw. It wasn't fair how good he looked. She wanted him out of her thoughts. It was better to think of a man that could never be hers than to let herself be overwhelmed by her present.

They passed through the open hanger down a hallway off to the right, making left and right turns until Miranda knew there was no way she was making it out of here without help. At some point in the journey, they came to an inner sitting area that had been carved from the walls.

The floor was a maze. Stone walls and half-doors came up to create cube-like spaces where people had desks for their holo-drives and other work. Miranda's eyes went wide. She had never seen so many people in one place in her whole life. Somehow, this place with its tight walls and underground spaces felt even fuller than the large city she had just come from. Both of which she had seen the first time that day. If her eyes got any wider, she would look like an Irentan. She couldn't believe she was seeing all of this.

All because of Oscar and his need for adventure. But if she had been with her family... She let that thought sit. She had no family, and saving Oscar had saved her. Longing for them was a death wish.

She wanted to be with them again. But she didn't want to go where they were anytime soon.

Eric kept pulling on her arm. He ushered her back through the cubicles to a door cut out of the wall. He opened the door, clicking on the lights. Inside, the room was twelve feet by twelve feet. A square cut to perfection. Except when she looked closer.

There were deep gouges on every wall. Something, some*one*, had desperately scratched the walls; probably trying to get out. Whoever they had shoved into this hole, and it certainly was a hole, either didn't need or was being denied light. And it had clearly driven them mad.

A shiver ran down Miranda's spine. This room in the middle of this hangar, inside this work area, was some kind of holding cell; maybe even a prison. She had never known any of this existed on her planet. She had never even thought to ask. All she knew was farm life. And farm life didn't include blasters and prison cells and spaceships.

Her whole world seemed to be cracking open with every step she took on this new adventure. Her mind stayed glued to the present, trying not to fracture under the pressure of her changing world. Miranda took a deep breath and looked away from the scratches.

A table sat in the center of the room. It looked like it came straight out of the floor, made by the same people that had carved the room. It matched the red-orange of the rock perfectly, and nearly blended in if she wasn't looking directly at it. On either side were two metal chairs. No frills or fancy carvings here; just a simple chair. The back stood up to about Miranda's waist.

On the left side corner, farthest away from the door, a small figure was curled up in a ball, its head in its knees. It looked to be a third-generation, humanoid droid; the warm glow of its silicone skin gave its age away.

Eric chose one of the chairs and pulled it out from underneath the table. A screech sounded as it scraped across the stone floor. He gestured for Miranda to sit. Miranda slid into the seat, aware that her dress was clinging to her.

The Ironside stepped back into the corner. Oscar, not wanting to be left out, slid across the threshold to a spot underneath the table.

"Beep beep beep beep beep beep," the little droid said. The humanoid droid looked up from his scrunched position. Whether it was truly a 'him' or 'her' was irrelevant. Humanoid droids didn't have any assigned sexual orientation. But the hair was short, the body stout, and it looked like something that would consider itself a 'he', if given the option. Not that MIranda was trying to judge it. She was just trying to keep from calling it an 'it' because she knew for a fact that Oscar did not like to be called an 'it'. There was some level of respect to be given a droid.

Miranda tried to smile, but she felt that maybe it looked more like a grimace.

"Please," she said, gesturing towards the chair in front of her. The droid uncurled slowly and stood up. Miranda could see where pieces of its silicone flesh been ripped, torn and bruised as he moved closer.

Metal wiring was visible underneath the patches of flesh and clothing that clung to his metal frame. Miranda looked it over. It could be a pleasure droid, or possibly a service droid. It was hard to tell.

It pulled out the chair in front of her, taking the time to lift it up so as not to screech across the stone floor, and sat hunched over before her.

The shoulders were broad. Fake silicone muscles outlined the arms. Its hands looked almost humanoid. Except for where gear joints showed through where knuckles should be.

Even with his head tucked, his eyes stared into hers. Red, as if on fire from the inside. They were the most inhuman eyes Miranda had ever seen in her entire life.

Miranda shifted in her chair. Oscar didn't have eyes. His sensors picked up a lot of things. But there was no facial expressions to anything that he did.

This droid was made to look and feel synonymous with the human beings that created it, only to suffer and deteriorate into its current state of disrepair.

"Ask him," the Ironside said from behind her. Miranda looked at Eric.

"Ask him what?"

Eric shrugged.

"Ask him," he said again.

IMPERIAL EDGE

Miranda rolled her eyes as she turned towards the droid. This interview was getting off to a great start.

"What is it that you need to tell us?" she said in the beeps and boops of droids. The droid didn't move. Miranda reached out a hand to pat his hand, not knowing what else to do.

"Beep Beep Boop," she said. *You have something to communicate?* The droid tilted his head to one side.

"Be bop bop bop," said the droid. *You talk funny. You are hard to understand.*

Miranda listened to his tones. They were less sharp than she was. Rounded at the edges. She adjusted in turn, trying to pick up his accent.

"Beep Beep Boop," she said again. She could tell that the way she spoke Droid to him was old fashioned. Like someone trying to speak Common from 50 years ago, not knowing how the language had shifted and changed on her home planet of a Oreilly 13.

"*You must tell me what you know so the Ironside will know.*" She kept adjusting her tone and trying to lift her words to match his. She had never spoken with any other droids outside of Oscar.

"Beep, beep." *This is going too slow,* complained Oscar from underneath the table.

The old droid looked briefly at Oscar. "Beep whistle bop," it said at last.

The Ironside tilted his helmet.

"What did he tell you?" he asked.

She turned back towards Eric.

"He told me Hello, and that his name is X5314,"

"Ask him where his charge is," Eric said. Miranda sighed and turned back towards the droid. She didn't like playing middle man. But she was here, and she had a job to do, apparently.

"*Where is your charge?*" She mouthed the syllables, trying to get the words to come out in the proper tone. While the Droid language was based off of Basic, each grade of droids had its own renditions and separate isms, adding symbols, set language, and other things so that the way and tone in which a beat or a box sounded, could change the meaning and structure of the words.

The droid paused for a minute, it's red eyes flaring for just a second. And then the lips shut over the top. Its head drooped, not meeting. Miranda's gaze.

"*Gone*," it said, the low tone registering with either guilt or shame. Miranda couldn't tell which.

The Ironside crossed his arms and looked intently at Miranda. She turned back towards him.

"He says his charge has been kidnapped." So sue her, she was exaggerating on the translation a bit, but she wanted to get more out of this Ironside who wouldn't even tell her what questions to ask.

"*Gone from my control,*" the droid continued.

Miranda translated for Eric.

"He said, taken out of his vicinity; that his charge is no longer his own." She added on that last part. But he had implied it with his last word. Or at least, that was one way to interpret Droid. That was her job in this space, after all.

The Ironside's helmet moved back and forth between the droid and the girl.

"What else? I need a location," Eric said.

"*No place,*" he said.

"*You can tell me. It is safe,*" Miranda said, trying to reassure the old droid, while at the same time coaxing him into telling her what the Ironside wanted.

"*No place I can go. No place for droid or human,*" he said back. Which wasn't really an answer. It was more like the expression of an emotion of giving up.

"*Where?*" Miranda said, emphasizing that she really needed the information. That all of this his surroundings, his imprisonment, wouldn't go away until he told her what the Ironside wanted to know.

The droid remained silent.

Miranda sighed. "He says that his charge has gone outside of his vicinity."

Eric let out a small curse.

"Who is this charge?" Miranda asked Eric.

The Ironside tilted his head helmet down at her. 'He must have put his helmet back on when we entered the room,' she thought to herself.

It had taken Miranda a while to register that fact. Everything here was so alien, she decided she liked him much better with the helmet. It made him separate, less human that way. It made it easier to deal with him.

"That is classified information," Eric said.

'Fine. It's classified information that I want to know,' Miranda thought.

"If you want to know any more information from this droid, then I need to know who his charge is. So that I know what to ask him," she said.

She was tired of this game. Tired of being dragged around and forced to do things. Her family was dead, her life was over. She was being kept from the next phase of her life because she had to speak Droid to apparently this droid that otherwise usually could speak human speak Common.

"What's wrong with him anyway?" she asked, trying to change the subject so that she could get back around to it.

"System Programming wiped," the Ironside said, starting to pace back and forth. "Rebels got hold of him and wiped his system access memory. They couldn't actually erase his programming memory. But they could erase his language settings. Now all he speaks is Droid." The Ironside raised his hand, pointing at the poor Third Gen droid.

"What's so special about this charge?" she asked again.

Eric sighed, exasperated.

"We just have to find him, pronto."

'So it was a *him*,' Miranda thought as she contemplated this newfound knowledge. So the droid had looked after someone important. Important enough to kill a whole family of farmers on an independent planet in the middle of the edge and cover it up, just so that no one would know the direction the rebels have been flying. Important enough to trouble with wiping a droid's language box when they didn't have the time to kill it. Or *couldn't* kill it. MIranda didn't know how hard it was to kill a droid. Pinning Oscar down for his yearly diagnostics was a pain. Every year they would draw straws for it. But not this year. From now on she was the straw. She shivered.

This must be one very important person. What were these rebels planning, and who was so important in all the galaxy that an Ironside team would be assigned to recapture them? Possibly a rebel leader? Or maybe even one of the royal family?

Miranda snapped her fingers.

"Who is your charge?" she asked the droid. She wasn't going to get it out of the Ironside, so she was going to get it out of this droid. Or she wasn't going to go one iota further on this journey.

"Beep Beep Boop," said the droid. Miranda's jaw dropped. There was no way. There was no possible way. The person that this droid was protecting was the Crown Prince.

Miranda's heart began to race. Her chest felt tight. Her head spun. If she wasn't careful the world would give way without her on it.

The Prince. No wonder they sent a troop of Ironsides on an interstellar chase across the galaxies against the rebels.

"Miranda," said Eric, his voice cutting through the noise in her head.

How could rebels even get their hands on the prince? Adamantium was the crown jewel of the Empire. A royal not just in name, but in action. His face adorned all of the holos, even in their small planetary farming community. Everyone knew what he looked like; what he had done. How he had saved all the planets during the Galactic wars. And his rise among the Ironsides to be one of the top military leaders of the day, all while still preparing to be Emperor.

"Miranda, what did he say? I need to know."

Mind you, everyone knew that the Senate ruled the Galactic them. The Emperor was more of a title, a tradition. Something to give credence to the old ways, so that others would know that there was a head to the snake. But it was a head without fangs. The Emperor had a say. He could speak in senate meetings and attend. But he had no vote.

They were a people's Empire. Each planetary outpost and galactic system sent representatives to the Senate. And even as far out here in the territories, they had representation. It was the way of the people to have a voice in the government. A say in the machine called The Empire.

The machine that kept everyone at peace, and together, and flowing. That kept planets being terraformed and new spaces being reached out to, galaxies reformed for human advancement. And now to know that someone had snatched the poor Prince right from wherever he had been serving; probably a battlefield.

Miranda shook her head. How in the world had she gotten involved in this? She needed to find out what has happened to the prince. Even as Eric asked, "Did he give you the planet's name?"

"No, I'll ask again," she told him.

"*What planet?*" Miranda said, trying to calm her facial expressions so as not to give away that she now knew. She knew who the target the Ironside was trying to protect was.

"Beep boop boop," the droid responded. Miranda looked at him, a frown at the corners of her mouth. She hadn't quite understood what he said.

"Beep beep bop," she said. *Please repeat.*

The droid remained silent. Oscar, on the other hand, got super excited under the table and started to beep frantically at her.

"Beep beep beep bop bop, beep beep beep bop bop," he yelled.

'Do SHUT UP Oscar,' she thought. Then she started to listen to what he was actually trying to communicate. It was the same sentence over and over again. Like a child trying to scream at its parent who wouldn't listen.

"Beep beep beep bop bop, beep beep beep bop bop," he repeated over and over again.

Miranda looked at Oscar.

"Alpha Carcerus." She said it out loud to make sure she was translating it right. The droid in front of her melted towards the floor. All the life in his mechanical parts seemed to dry up in a rush. At that exact moment Oscar squealed with joy at being heard. Eric swung Miranda's chair around. Her knees banged into the stone leg of the desk.

"Ouch," she said. That was going to leave a bruise.

"Did you say Alpha Carcerus?" He pronounced each syllable, making sure that she heard him.

"Ouch. Like I said, Yes. That's what Oscar said."

Eric looked down at the little droid. If a droid without a face could stick its tongue out at someone, that's what Oscar would have been doing at that exact moment.

"Not him." Eric pointed to the pile of parts that used to be a living, if not breathing, droid.

"Yes, that is what I said." Miranda was getting tired of this back and forth.

"We need to go. Now." Eric grabbed her by the arm and pulled. Miranda looked at him, puzzled.

"What is that place? And why do we need to go now?" she asked. Eric just gave her one last look before yanking her fully out of the chair and towards the door. "And what about him?" she said, pointing back to the droid.

"The forces here will take care of it," Eric said.

"But..." Miranda protested.

"He needs a reboot and a redesign. We couldn't afford to do that before. But now that we have all the information we need..."

Miranda pulled back from Eric so she could stare at him. He was halfway in and out of the door.

"I'm still confused."

Eric sighed.

"Look, it's relatively simple. With the help of your Oscar, we have a planetary name. We know where they've taken the prisoner," he said. Miranda nodded her head, her arms still crossed. Exasperation still on her face.

"There's no time to waste here."

On that they both agreed, but Miranda wanted to make sure she wasn't running towards certain death, lead by someone without even a notion of a plan.

She looked back at the pile of droid. And ahead at the Ironside. Those were her two options: staying in this room with a lifeless droid in the dark, or going on whatever adventure that lay ahead on this planet that seemed to scare the life out of this droid. It was a hard choice. But she moved towards the door anyways.

"All right. Let's go."

Chapter 10

Miranda strapped herself into the seat. First, she had to maneuver the large belt buckles with heavy metal clips attached to synthetic fabrics she'd never felt before. Once fastened in, her hands found a home gripping the handlebars on either side of the seat.

It was a good thing no one else wanted to hold them. Her left side was empty, but Eric sat to her right. He made no move to remove her hand from the handle. In fact, he wasn't really moving at all.

It was her first time riding in a shuttle off planet. Even the idea of leaving the place where she was born, the only home that she had ever known, was beyond her imagination of just a week ago. It now seemed incredibly hard. All she wanted to do was to close her eyes and wake up back in her warm, comfy bed with her quilted blanket that her mother had made. She opened her eyes. She was still in the shuttlecraft.

A pilot sat at the helm; his badge said that his name was Rycer. Two regular army infantry soldiers sat on the shuttle guns to the left and right of him. Miranda hadn't gotten a good look at their badges as they traveled up off planet to the waiting starship that would carry them on the next leg of their journey. Eric sat next to her, and another Ironside sat across from him. Both of them looked relaxed, possibly asleep again.

Miranda smirked. 'Wouldn't it be great just to hide your expressions and all of your emotions behind a helmet?' she thought. She couldn't wait until she had passed all the tests and gotten to that helmet to hide behind. Then, and only then, could she probably sleep on an aircraft like this instead of being so freaked out that the idea of rest had completely abandoned her.

"You okay back there?" asked one of the gunners.

"Yeah, fine," said Miranda, feeling anything but. The glint off his red uniform as he turned towards he made her smile involuntarily. The Ironside across from her caught the smile.

"You know why regular military wear all red," he said.

"No," Miranda confessed. This was the second time she'd ever seen a regular military officer. She hadn't even remembered that they wore red, or if it had been a part of her holo lessons.

"It's to hide the blood stain."

"Whose blood?" Miranda asked, not sure if she wanted the answer.

"Why, the rebels we blow up, of course," said the soldier.

At the same time the Ironside said, "Theirs, of course."

Miranda tried to keep the confusion off her face, but some of it must have shown through because both of them broke out into laughter. She could feel the red creep up her face.

"My name's Gunther, but everyone calls me Cash," the gunner said, reaching out a hand for her to clasp. She reached hers out awkwardly. She'd heard about off worlders clasping hands, but no one in her family did it. When her hand fumbled to repeat the moves his made, more red burned on her face.

"I think we met before," she finally stammered out.

"Oh?" The soldier sounded amused.

"Yeah. At a bride auction."

The soldier laughed. "Sorry, I'm not in the market for one of those!" Then he turned back around.

'This is going to be a long flight,' she thought, just as the shuttle landed with a thump.

Miranda loosened her grip on the handles. That was quick. They hadn't been in the air for more than a few minutes at the most. Not even enough time for her to feel the weight of leaving her planet behind.

She felt herself lift off the floor for a few seconds before the gravitational simulator on the flight deck kicked in. For the perfect of moments she was flying; then her stomach hit the floor and her body felt heavier than normal. Then everything went up again to a normal feeling. She shook her head to try and clear it.

She looked around the transport. Eric looked like he was still sleeping, the bump of landing not even phasing his relaxed pose. The other Ironsides all remained the same. Nothing new to them. Miranda tucked that information away. She'd have to get used to the gravitational shifts between planet and space.

That's when the real wait happened. Miranda lost track of the time as they sat inside the belly of the starship, waiting to be let on board. It was a good thing they didn't have to wait in orbit for all the paperwork it took to land one of these things. First, they had to wait for the pilot to give all the necessary call signs. There were a lot of call signs. Strings of numbers that left Miranda's head spinning. Then came the paperwork. Each member of the crew had to confirm their identity on the roster and fill out a questionnaire.

"This is how we tell the rebel ships from the Empire ships," Cash informed her. Miranda's ears perked up.

"They bury every landing in paperwork, knowing that any rebel forces bent on taking over a ship would give up halfway through, override the system, and burst forth to find themselves trapped and fired upon."

"For real?" Miranda asked. The other Ironside nodded his head in agreement.

"Every word," he said, the sound coming out through his helmet crisp as if it got cooked and then fed out a speaker.

"And when we're done with the paperwork?" she asked.

"Then the real fun happens," Cash supplied.

"The real fun?" Miranda asked.

"Yeah," he said. "We get decontaminated."

Miranda gave him a puzzled look. Eric leaned forward.

"We get a twenty four hour decontamination cell," he supplied.

"Oh," Miranda said, sitting back in her seat. She tried to look like that didn't scare her. That she knew that coming off planet, you needed to be in decontamination for twenty four hours. Normal procedures that she'd never heard of before today.

"By then we should be in orbit," Eric supplied.

"So we aren't going to really get to be on the ship?" Miranda asked. Eric finished typing in what he needed to fill out on the holo and handed it to her.

"It's super easy. Just fill out what you can; put your finger here... That's right."

He guided her hands over the keys, showing her how to fill out the forms. One box after another. This was definitely one way to kill patience. If she'd been part of a rebel team she would have given up and stormed the ship by now.

"The hyperspace trip is only fourteen hours from here," Eric said.

"That's close." She marked another box. They were to the Yes or No questions. Like had she ever had an ingrown toenail. Did she menstruate, and if so, when was the last time. Was she covered in unnecessary spots. She made sure to check no on that one, not knowing what necessary spots would look like, but unwilling to want to find out.

"So we will be in decom the entire time," Eric finished.

"Saves time if we don't wait," Cash supplied. All the men made the same grunt noise at the same time.

Miranda clicked another box. When was this form ever going to end, and did they really need to know if she had been attacked by an ors in the last 24 hrs? The answer was 'No', but still, what difference did it make?

"There, just sign here and initial there, and..." Eric took the holo from her. He looked it over and pressed one more button. "There. All done."

The doors to the landing bay separated, providing a narrow path from the shuttles' exit ramp to a hole in the hull. The air shimmered between them and the rest of the landing bay. Miranda squinted her eyes and reached out to try to get a better view through it. Shock ran down her arm.

"Ouch," she said. The word left her mouth before she thought better of it.

"Force field; be careful, little miss," Cash said.

Miranda huffed. Ignoring whatever lay on the other side of the force field, she pushed past the chuckling Ironside and Cash, catching up with the pilot. At least he hadn't made fun of her yet.

The forcefield corridor emptied out on a set of double doors that connected to a pair of rooms. One was clearly for sleeping, since it was made up of bunk beds like the ones in the kids room at her parents' house. The other had couches for sitting and a video screen, probably to provide some level of entertainment. Everything was encased in a layer of synthetic material that reminded Miranda of plastic, but it felt softer and less porous somehow.

"There is a shower in the bathroom off the cabin," said the pilot, Rycer. "You may use it to get changed."

"Thanks," said Miranda. As she rose Oscar got tangled in her legs. She stumbled forward. Eric caught her by her arm and steadied her before she landed on the floor. Miranda ducked her head and headed for the bathroom.

The shower was pure heaven. Back on the farm they just had a wash tub that was used for animals and humans alike. There had been a shower room a generation back, but the reconstitutional pump had gone out back between the birth of her aunt Mary and her Uncle Maximus. No one had ever seen fit to pay for the replacement.

This was the first time in her life she'd ever washed in a true shower. The steam hit her first, warming her to the bone. It cleaned out her nasal passages and crept into every corner of her body. Then came the cold water. It poured over her like the holos of waterfalls on the pleasure planets in the corridors of the Empire. Back where the senators and other high officials took their Holy Days to commune with God.

The torrent of water scraped every part of her clean. For a moment she felt like she might drown under the pressure of the water. Then it stopped and a warm heat filled the room. Just warm enough to lift the water from her skin and hair, but not warm enough to be hot or make her sweat. As she exited dry and clean of all the dirt and blood that had clung to her, the shower spritzed her with a light jasmine scent. Like her mother's favorite tea.

"Thank you for your service faithful friend," she told the blue dress before sticking it into the recycle container. Her arms went to give it a hug, but her nose stopped her. Now that she was clean, the smell of death from the dress overwhelmed her. No wonder Cash didn't want to get anywhere near her. She would have run from her, too.

She quickly braided her hair. Then she twisted it into a tight bun on her head, securing it with the bracelet she carried on her wrist for this purpose. Then she changed into the uniform she'd stashed in Oscar and made her way back into the hanger.

She walked in to find the three of them in a heated conversation. They must have heard her because when she got close enough to hear all three stopped talking.

Eric coughed. They all turned her way. Cash's eyes widened and then narrowed into a frown. Miranda wondered what Cash saw that upset him. Rycer whistled.

Miranda pulled at the vest. It was tight holding her all in.

"I didn't know that med showers could turn a terran stellar," Rycer joked. Eric and the other Ironside remained still, their expressions unmoved. Cash grimaced.

"Not cool man," Cash said. "Not cool at all. Some of us are terran born."

Miranda kept walking. She did not like the way they stared at her.

"Come on, Stellar, take a seat next to me; I'll be your creche Pop," Rycer jeered. Miranda slumped past, trying to make her body as small as possible. "What? You only got eyes for the Irons, Sweet Cheeks?" he continued on. Miranda glanced back. Rycer slapped his lap as if he wanted her to sit on it. She kept walking.

"I said, not cool," Cash said, slapping Rycer upside the head.

"Get your dirty terran hands off me," Rycer said back. He shoved Cash.

"Cresh you," Cash retorted, shoving Rycer back into his chair. Rycer lunged at Cash, tackling him to the floor. Miranda watched as the two men rolled around like her brothers. Fists flew. A spray of blood splattered the floor from where Cash's elbow hit Rycer's face.

"Enough," Eric said. Both men stopped mid swing. They separated from each other, preferring to back away. Rycer wiped the blood off his lip. Cash's eye started to show signs of swelling. The two men sat on either sides of Eric. Rycer's arms were locked in from of him; Cash's were open in a 'Come and get me, I dare you' pose.

Between the shower and the fight, they were one hour down with many more to go. Miranda made the decision to spend it sleeping. She hadn't gotten a good rest since the morning she'd chased Oscar up the mountain. Now felt like the best time to do just that.

Miranda walked past thier gaping eyes into the bunk bed room, grabbed a blanket and pillow off the wall, and collapsed into the first open bed she saw. Sleep overtook her the second her head hit the pillow. Just like that, she was out.

"Beep, beep!" Oscar yelled in her ear. Miranda stretched. She'd been dreaming of playing fort with Michael. The two of them were Ironsides on a mission to save the galaxy. It had felt so real; the heat of the sun on her back as they chased rebel tibbers through the field.

"What do you want?" Miranda asked, her eyes still closed with sleep. She rubbed them, displacing the salt crystals that had formed around them in the night. She opened her eyes to give the little droid a good stare only to come face to face with an Ironside mask.

She sat up with a start, her head colliding with the rail of the bunk above her. Pain shot through her head. At least she didn't say 'Ouch' this time. Either she was getting used to the pain or she was getting better at hiding it.

"Good, you're awake."

She knew that voice. A name floated up to her from the haze of sleep and pain.

"Here, eat this; as soon as I talk to the captain we are leaving."

Miranda took what he was holding out to her. It looked like a bar of black goo. She took a bite. It was gritty, but not so bad tasting that she couldn't swallow. She took another bite, then another until it was gone.

She noticed that she hadn't taken her new uniform off when she went to sleep. It was rumbled but otherwise looked no different.

"Thanks," she said.

"You're welcome," he said. "Come on, we all need to be in the briefing room."

Miranda tried to pay attention. It was all so boring. She wasn't awake enough yet. Even with whatever that bar had been, she missed the fresh farm milk and her mother's pancakes. The smell of which could wake the dead in a good way.

"Sir, I understand that this ship is your priority, but in regard to this mission, I maintain all authority," Eric stated.

Miranda suppressed a yawn.

"You will not leave orbit. You will not call for backup. You will maintain contact until we have succeeded in our mission."

"I am the captain of this ship," the captain said through his little holo image, shaking with rage. Miranda read his title along the base of his projected image. Captain Rocford J Pendelton of the ERSS Altitude.

Miranda blinked and read it again. Yep. Whoever this captain was, he was from the Pendleton system. Pendleton was one of the third ranked systems in the outer edge of the second wave of Imperial terraforming. Not so high up in the food chain to feel safe from an Ironside taking over. But not so low as to be someone who climbed the rungs of the ladder, inch by inch, from a farming community like hers. She filed that information away for later. Right now it was just starting to get good.

"And I have been given papers from the Imperial senate," Eric said, the ice in his voice a final word.

Rocford ground his teeth. "I cannot allow my ship to take part in your suicide mission."

"If you are done filing our paperwork, accept your orders and release my craft," Eric stated.

"Sir, yes sir," Captain Rocford said at last.

Chapter 11

It didn't take much effort on Miranda's part to see that it was forced words. Especially the way the Captain spit out the word 'sir' before clicking off the holo.

"So we're going off planet?" she asked Eric.

"No," he said, correcting her. "We are going down *to* the planet." They were already off planet. This was a spaceship. Miranda's cheeks reddened.

She looked over at all of the other guys. None of them looked too thrilled at the destination. Did they even know what it was? The fight with the Captain, him calling it a suicide mission, certainly didn't help with morale.

"Okay, fine," she replied. "But I don't get it." Then she remembered who this mission was to protect: the crown prince. Her family had died over this.

"Rebels," she said. He nodded his agreement.

"Why am I here?" she asked. "I'm just a recruit; I haven't even been to basic yet!"

Eric paused for only a moment. "You speak Droid. Nobody else who can is close enough to get here in time."

'I'm getting nowhere with this guy,' Miranda thought. She switched tactics.

"What's so special about this planet, anyways?" She asked Eric as they headed back through the corridor. She made sure not to touch the edges. She didn't want another shock.

"We'll talk about once we are in flight," Eric replied. His tone was quiet and resolute. " I don't want any of our mission leaking through." Eric pointed at the cameras.

They'd been watching them this whole time. They may have not made it out of quarantine, but they were still being watched. Miranda shut her mouth. If Eric thought it wasn't safe to talk about, then it wasn't safe to talk about, end of story. She loaded herself back into the shuttle, clicked in her belt and waited. The pilot was the last to get on, making extra motions with the gear controls before lifting off the launch pad.

'Here we go,' Miranda thought. The ride had been so smooth, Coming up to the spaceship, the movements of the ship so smooth, her sleep so deep. She hadn't thought anything about space travel so far.

It was odd.

It felt like just being in another building on the planet. She couldn't even feel the rumblings or the sliding that kept her grounded. But when the shuttle craft started to spin, her knuckles went from her relaxed posture to seat-gripping white again.

"What were you going to say? About the mission being suicidal?" she yelled at Eric over a loud whistling sound.

IMPERIAL EDGE

Perchunk. Something hit into the side of the craft. The pilot swerved left, then right.

What were they doing going through an astro field? They were supposed to be doing a planetary landing.

"What could hit shielding this hard and not simply bounce off?" said Cash. He grabbed his gun and shot off another volley of rounds to break up the debris before contact. "Almost feels like we're on a roller coaster, and not hurtling at high speeds towards a planet!"

"Report!" Eric shouted at the pilot.

"Interplanetary shielding, sir," Rycer replied. "We're bouncing off of pieces of interstellar debris and old ships." He didn't need to add the lines that the ship had failed to dock. Everyone in the shuttle got the picture.

"I don't think we're going to make it," screamed the pilot.

"Keep on course, Pilot," Eric said in his commanding Ironside tone.

The pilot held on for dear life.

"Sir, it's ripping the shuttle apart, sir."

"Did you enter the code line I gave you?"

"Sir, Yes, sir. It doesn't seem to be operational." He turned his head back to respond to Eric. The controls shook in his hands. Another round of debris smashed into the side of the ship. "The Gate isn't opening up."

Miranda flew six inches into the air, caught in her upper harness, and was slammed back down. Every bone in her body rattled from her teeth down to her feet. She was thankful for the arm holds now, which seemed to be her lifeline as they plummeted towards their destination. Rycer kept swerving.

"I'm gonna be sick," said the other gunner. Miranda was right there with him.

The one galactic fair that came to their small town on a Oreilly 13 had what is known as roller coasters and wurly do's and other fast paced Interstellar technology rides. It all seemed fun, with just a touch of life threatening danger. But compared to this, they were tame.

Miranda slid, trying to release the tension that built up in her arms and neck from holding on so tight. Her nails bit into her palms, leaving little red crescent shaped indentations. They were going to make it. She knew that they were going to make it.

Eric swore. The curse echoed off the walls of the shuttle.

"What do you mean the code's not working?"

"I said the code's not working, sir," replied the pilot.

"It was given to me by the Imperial notification chain itself," Eric said.

"I recognize that, sir," said the pilot. "That doesn't mean that it is operational."

IMPERIAL EDGE

Eric somehow made his way towards the panicked pilot, step by slow step. Seconds turned into hours as the craft spiraled out of control, bouncing around like an apple in a bucket of water.

The wall seemed to be creaking in around them, pounding in from all sides. There was a sudden shift as the pilot swerved to the left, veering off course to avoid another round of volleys.

Eric slammed into the right wall, landing in Cash's lap.

"Get off," Cash said, pushing Eric up off him and towards the pilot. Miranda watched as he claimed the last three steps.

"Scoot over" Eric ordered. The pilot shifted as much as he could without letting go of the controls.

Eric punched something into the control panel. His hands flew from one control to the next in a pattern of movements Miranda's eyes couldn't follow.

"Sir," Rycer said, looking up at him.

"Shut up and do your job," Eric replied.

"Sir!" the pilot said again, looking ahead.

A large gate the size of a planet loomed in front of them. Steal and iron, and brobanium, shifting and clasping on the vid screen. Every sensor in the ship was screaming that there was a big metal thing dead ahead and they were flying straight towards it.

"Do not veer," Eric roared.

Rycer went to veer left, disregarding the direct order. Eric knocked him out, took hold of the controls and centered them on the big sphere.

Miranda put her hands over her head and ducked down to her knees. If they were going to crash into whatever it was, she wanted to be in the crash position.

They flew dead center into the large, luminous object.

Miranda waited for that moment when her life would flash before her eyes. She had read about it on holos, heard about it from friends who had slipped beneath the ice, skating on the ponds and been rescued by a dry out team. She'd never thought that she would experience it. Life on O'reilly 13 was hard, but not necessarily deadly.

Well, at least it hadn't been before. Before the rebels. The rebels took a hard, but rewarding life and turned it into an impossible one. One full of danger and death for no good reason.

Instead of her life flashing before her eyes, she saw a warm table, comforting food and the work of being a farmer's wife evaporate in front of her. Everything she'd spent her life dreaming about becoming slipped into a mist of planetary debris. Then nothing.

She waited. Nothing happened. She could still feel her breath pouring in and out of her lips. She opened her eyes.

The ship was fine. Dented in places, but whole and holding. She had eyes to see it through. They glided over the planet, no longer stuck in the upper atmosphere.

"Take this piece of useless junk out of my seat," Eric shouted back at the crew. The other Ironside slipped wordlessly up, grabbed the pilot by his shoulders and pulled him back to where the rest of them were in the shuttle. Then he strapped the guy into a seat before strapping himself in.

Eric took over the pilot's place at the helm. Miranda smiled. An uncontrolled giggle erupted from inside her. The laughter was caught by Cash. Soon everyone in the craft was laughing uncontrollably, the tension gone.

"Shuttlecraft to base. Shuttlecraft to landing base, do you read me?" Eric said into the coms. Something dinged back.

"Welcome travelers. Shuttle bay 6 is ready and waiting for your arrival," said a sweet sounding voice. It had the broken gate of a prerecorded AI track, with just a tinge of inhumans that came from old system controls. Eric typed up the trajectory and started the system into the run.

Miranda watched as they descended towards the landing pad. Sludge clouds cut like butter as they moved closer to the planet's surface. Then it parted into a dark rain. A lightning bolt split the sky, revealing landing pad 6. That's when she noticed it: the disarray of broken pieces of shuttle craft littering the landing bay.

Eric swore. He tried to lift up on the controls to get out of the landing pattern, but it was too late. The Autopilot Landing System on the shuttle had kicked in. For the second time in less than 20 minutes. Miranda feared for her life.

Chapter 12

Miranda watched the world tear apart in slow motion. As she turned, end over end, pieces of the craft broke apart. Shattered glass shards sprayed the air, lacerating her face. She fell forward with the motion of the shuttle. Up, then down, then forward, up and down again. Bits of crushed vid screens whipped past her head. Metal gears and tubing sprayed streams of dangerous chemicals. She leaned back enough for one to shoot past her. The green liquid melted a hole in the side of the ship.

Chunk.

The spaceship hit something, momentarily freezing the spinning wreck. Then there was a large screech that felt like it came from her very bones. Miranda hung upside down, held in by her straps. She watched in horror as the other half of the ship split in front of her eyes. Down into the darkness it went. The knocked unconscious pilot, the other Ironside, and the second gunner unit fell with it.

There was another long groan as the ship settled into its new weight. Mirand flipped back over with it as it rested on the platform. She sat back, panting,

"You're still alive," she told herself. "You're still alive." When she felt like she could breathe again she unhooked herself from the harness that kept her from being a pinball inside an oxandon machine.

"Eric," she called into what had once been a cockpit. Now it was scrap metal.

"Oscar," she cried. Her little droid had not been secured. He had gone up to bother Eric during the landing. She lifted piece of metal and scraps of things to see if he was trapped or hiding. She stopped every couple of feet to listen for his whine or Eric's breathing. Oscar was nowhere to be found.

At the cockpit, Miranda found Eric still sitting in the pilot seat. His harness had kept him in place. But his helmet had come off in all the shuffling, and he had a laceration across his forehead.

She searched him for any other bumps and bruises. But he seemed to just have been knocked out by something. There were multiple puncture marks through the shuttle craft's front window, so it could have been anything.

Miranda made her way over to the gunner seat on what was left of her side of the craft. Cash lay there in a pool of blood, a trickle of it coming from his mouth; his eyes wide in shock.

A piece of some craft penetrated through the middle of his chest. Miranda suppressed a gag by covering her mouth and stepping back. It was like looking at her parents' dead bodies all over again.

She turned and put her head between her legs, trying to breath, trying to get a semblance of normalcy back. She needed to get over this she needed to overcome death. Least Eric was still alive, even if he was unconscious.

She looked for the other Ironside and the pilot. And the other gun gunner. But all three of them had been on the other side of the craft and gone down wherever it had gone. Miranda made her way out of the debris.

"Oscar!" She cried, not knowing any of the other names of her companions.

She should have known. At least then she could have prayed for them, or mourn their loss.

She stood there on the tarmac looking out over everything that just happened. The only conscious survivor of the crash.

She was so wrapped up in her need to find Oscar, or someone that could help her with Eric, that she didn't notice the phazer fire until she felt the shock of it hit her body, followed by the wave of pain as she passed out.

Miranda's eyes felt glued shut. The kind of stuck that hours and hours of sleep building up on the edges and corners could only accomplish. Her head still hurt were the blast that had knocked her out. The bruises and cuts from bouncing around in the shuttle craft had every area of her body transmitting pain to the point that her brain had just blocked it down to an overall dull ache. She felt bruised and battered. She just hoped she wasn't bleeding anymore.

Slowly, she lifted her fingers and rubbed them against the salt on her eyes. She opened them to the world around her.

White completely filled her vision. Miranda blinked again.

There was nothing. Had she died and gone to heaven? Or was this hell?

Miranda hope that she wasn't in hell. She'd been a believer her entire life. She had never questioned the prophecies or the reality of the galactic transmission. And now all around her was proof of something. She just needed to find out what.

The white was bright, almost blinding, with just enough dark to cause her to squint but not have to shut her eyes again. She removed more sleep from her eyes. She picked out the bigger chunks from the corners, then blinked a couple of times to get used to the new light. Then she tried to look around again.

'Well, if this is Heaven, it is pretty lonely,' she thought. She had always been told that all of her friends and family, all of the people that she loved most dear, would be with her there. They were all believers, too.

Miranda started walking ahead into the light to see if she could find someone.

Bam. Her face collided with something hard. She put her hands forward to see what her eyes had missed. It felt hard under her touch. She ran her hands up and down as far as she could reach. It remained the same solid hard surface. She counted back her steps. She had taken about about five steps before she had hit the wall.

There was no way to tell what kind of wall it was she had run into. Everything around her was endless white in all directions.

She thought she could have walked for hours. But no; there she was, pressing up against something. Her hands felt around for a panel or a door. Anything that would separate the white from the white. But there was nothing.

She turned around and walked the other direction. A little less than 10 paces later she hit another wall. She could feel it under her fingertips. Smooth as plastic and bright, but not cold or particularly warm. Nor did it shock like the force field on the ship during decontamination. This was something different. Like being trapped inside a light bulb.

Miranda thought about it and walked five paces to what she now considered the middle of the room, turned, then headed in the other direction.

Five paces. She ran dab smack into another wall. This time she did it at a good pace and smacked her forehead into the thing. The force of it sent her back onto her butt, where she sat staring up at the blank whiteness, realizing that it had no depth, even though it looked out onto eternity.

"This is definitely not Heaven," she said to herself; and she hoped, very, very badly, that it wasn't Hell, either.

"Is anyone there?" she yelled into the blankness. No response. "My name is Miranda Farmer, and I would like to know where I am." Still sitting on her bottom, Miranda used her heels to turn around again, and looked back at another blank white space. She leaned her head back against the wall.

"How do you know if you're dead or not?" she asked the wall. She had this growing suspicion that if she were dead, she wouldn't feel like a big bruise. Somehow she had always envisioned death with a perfect body. One that never aged, never got cuts, never got hurt, stayed whole. And, well, it might have pain, but not like this.

Actually, no; she believed in Heaven that there wouldn't be any pain because you couldn't get scratched or cut or bleed out or hurt yourself. And she looked down at the bloody mess that was her new uniform. She had been cut to shreds in the crash. She was 100% sure that this was not an afterlife.

"So where am I?" she thought out loud. She knew for one thing that this place was made to look endless, but was in fact, a 10 foot by 10 foot square. And the only thing that she knew that was 10 foot by 10 foot and looked like eternity was a prison cell. They had been part of her holo lessons. Massive planetoids good for nothing else but storing the living dead back before the Enlightenment.

Now, anyone who committed a serious crime was punished in one of two ways. Some were given the option to go into service for the Empire. This could include builder work, military work, mining, or even terraforming. All were very dangerous and deadly jobs. The likelihood of coming back before paying off a debt was very small, but at least it was a life.

The other option for those that could not be trusted to be around others was simply death. Miranda had never been to one of the public executions. Before, when a person was found to have taken more than one life simply for the joy of it, they were paraded out in front of the entirety of the video screens of the Empire and given a chance to repent for their sins against humanity and the lives that they took needlessly. Then they would be promptly sent on to the next life. Two wrongs, and all that. At least this way they did not have a chance to redeem themselves.

It was sad, really, she thought. There are some people who take life from others and not seek to atone for it.

She shook her head. The Empire had gotten rid of prisons over 200 years ago.

During the great Age of Enlightenment, it was determined that there was no crime that was unredeemable. In fact, every crime, every act of violence against another, had been laid out in a code and given a price value that the person would have to pay back to the individual in question. If the person was unable to pay it back, that's when service to the Empire was instituted. It would provide the person in question a job to pay the other person back, a roof over their head, food on the table, and oversight so that they could redeem themselves for their actions. And no dollar amount was ever set higher than the life of the person who was meant to pay it. That's why prison planets like the one that they were traveling to had gone empty and into disrepair.

So to be in a prison cell was something Miranda never thought would happen to her in her life. It just couldn't happen. But here she was.

"Hello, is anyone there?" Miranda called at the walls. She was tired of pacing them. But she wasn't tired anymore. She checked the cuts and bruises around her body. Nothing was bleeding. Everything had been washed clean.

"I would really like to know where I am," she asked again. No noise reached her ears. If this kept up she would start to think herself mad. She sighed. She was getting nowhere. Whatever this light was, whatever this room was, it dampened all of her senses. And it was starting to drive her insane.

She took a deep breath, closed her eyes, and focused on her breathing. Who knew how long she had been here? Maybe everything had become hopeless.

Her cuts had healed to a light red. Her bruises to pink dots. It was possible that she had been here for hours, or days, or even weeks, judging by how closed up her cuts were. Or the other possibility was that whatever this place could heal the human body faster than normal. It could have been designed for that, but there was no way for Miranda to know. If this was a med pod on a prison planet, these things were meant to torture and to keep their occupants alive. But if that was the case, where was the food and water?

Miranda looked around. She was thirsty. She her tongue against her lips. Her mouth was dry, and her lips were cracked and bleeding from dehydration.

"I miss you so much, Oscar." she said in Droid. The lights seemed to dim, and then return to its off-putting whiteness. Miranda tried to stop the tears that were sitting at the corners of her eyes. But there just wasn't enough moisture in her body to cry.

Her stomach growled. Who knows how long it had been since she had last eaten. If they didn't feed her, or bring her drink soon... well, there might not be a body to find. Miranda shuttered at the thought. No, she wasn't going die here. Not when she had survived the crash. Not when she had survived the interrogation of that droid. Not when she had survived the rebels who had killed all of her family. The rebels deserved to pay for what they had done. And she was the only one alive left to do it. She would find a way out of here. She would find her droid. And she would kick those rebels back to their planetary home worlds.

Miranda took a deep breath.

"Close your eyes and think," she said. There had to be commands, had to be some way to feed prisoners and let them in and out of the room. She hadn't gotten here all on her own. Even if she had fallen through the ceiling, which she was now betting was only 10 feet above her head, there still had to be some sort of entrance into this place. Miranda felt around the walls again, searching for any edges or cracks anything that might even feel like a door, or drawer, or something. She painstakingly went around every inch of the room, her fingers lightly gliding in all directions. At last, after what seemed like hours, she had still found nothing.

She sat back down again.

"Think, Miranda, think!" she said. If Oscar was here, she could run all of her ideas by him. If she had Oscar, she could use his sensory base to look through whatever these walls were and find out where the control panel was. Then she could use his laser cutter to break through this to the outside, or whatever it went to. And then plug him in and use his system accesses to open the doors. But Oscar wasn't there. She just had her.

And what was she good at doing?

"Droid. I can speak Droid," she said to the walls. Miranda started talking at the walls "If this is a prison planet, then most likely the cells are operated by the computer system."

"Please pull up the computer mainframe," she asked it.

Nothing.

She thought again.

"Beep bop, bop, bop, bop, bop, bop, bop bop." She felt the Droid words flowing off her tongue in the she accent had spoken in the interrogation room. If this truly was a prison planet, then it had to be at least two hundred years old, if not older. And Miranda had a feeling that this particular prison planet was much, much older. It might have even predated the Empire. And If that was the case, then they probably spoke Droid that was even older than Oscar. Not that Miranda thought that was possible.

"Beep beep boop," Miranda tried it again. This time emphasizing her words. *I want to speak to the mainframe.*

"Beep booooooooooooooooooooooo." The long, slow words echoed off the walls. Miranda had to put her hands over her ears to block the sound. It made the walls vibrate, it was so loud.

"Be bop," she replied back. She couldn't quite tell what it said because of the way the words reverberated through the room. It might have said, "Hi there," or, "What do you want?"

So she told it what she wanted back.

"Open Door," she said in Droid. A panel slid open and a drawer was in front of her. Inside was what looked like pellet food: an old rationing system that never went bad and could be packed on to old interstellar transport ships. These often would take three to four light years to reach their destinations. Next to the food was what looked like a water box.

She stuck the straw through the metallic sealed opening and drank. She didn't care if it was poisoned or not. All she cared about was the fact that it was liquid and it was on her tongue. She swallowed the food pills. They tasted like nothing, but they were filling. And that's what mattered.

"Beep Beep," she told the computer. *Thank you. Now a door, please.* She believed that the thing had heard 'drawer' instead of 'door' the first time.

A panel in the wall popped forward and slid to the side, revealing a dark corridor without. Miranda excitedly stepped forward and stuck her head in and down the corridor. She had to be careful. Whatever had caught her and brought her here was probably wandering these halls. She hadn't seen it, or knew how it operated. So she didn't know what she faced entering that corridor.

"I've got to find Oscar and Eric and the crew," she thought as she made her way carefully down the hall.

She checked every couple of feet. There was a door like hers, sunk slightly back from the main hallway. And each, to her surprise, had a control panel that registered whether or not a prisoner was being kept inside. With a few tweaks, she was able to press the controls and find out if each room was occupied without opening the doors. It took time; precious time that she didn't know if she had or not, to check each and every room. And eventually she came to a split in the corridor where the cells went left and right. She had to make a decision. Left or right. "What would have you done?" she asked in Droid to Oscar.

But he was not there to guide her. The big booming beeps of the computer sounded again. But this time without reverberating around the walls of the room. They weren't quite as deafening.

"Right," she said. It was telling her to go right. Miranda turned and walked swiftly down the hallway. This one only had one door in the middle of a long corridor. It was odd; these rooms seemed to be bigger. Less individual cells, and more something else. Halfway down the corridor she found the control panel and checked.

There was one single, solitary life inside. Maybe it was Eric, or maybe it was someone or some*thing* else. She had no way of knowing for sure. And the only way to find out who it was was to open the door.

Miranda's hand shook over the panel. She'd come this far. If it was Eric, he'd been badly injured the last time she saw him. So it was important that she find out if he was ok. She heard a clicking sound coming down the hall. She turned just in time to see the outline of a shadow approaching her position. She pressed the sequence that would open the door, desperate to get out of the hall. Anything trapped in there couldn't be worse than being recaptured by whatever was out here.

Chapter 13

The panel slid open with a soft click. This place was noticeably quiet for being old and in disrepair. The doors here were well oiled. None of them squeaked. It was another mystery that she would someday solve, but that day was not today.

Careful not to be spotted, she slipped into a room that looked identical to hers. Four walls of empty nothingness. She stepped forward into the room. The outside panel had said there was a prisoner in here, but she didn't see anything but the white. She went to take a step forward and tripped over a body. A person lay motionless on the floor.

Their feet entangled. Their limbs splayed out. She fell flat on top of her Ironside.

"Eric!" she cried. She wrapped her arms around him, giving him a big hug. The fact that she was laying on top of him was forgotten in the joy of finding him alive.

"I'm just so glad I found you," she said.

"Well hello, little butterfly," Eric said.

'Little butterfly?' Miranda thought. That was new. Maybe him hitting his head in that crash was more than she'd thought.

"Who might you be?" Eric's face stared back at her with a blank expression. The handsome lines, the flowing hair. The perfect jaw. Everything was there. But none of scrapes or bruises or blood from when she had last seen him in the cockpit marred his face.

Blush crept up her own face as she realized that she was pinning him to the floor.

"Oh! Sorry," she said as she scrambled up off of him.

"It's okay. I much like my daydreams molesting me." He wiggled his eyes at her. Miranda started, her mouth coming open on its own accord.

"I'm not..." she stuttered. "I wasn't..." The words refused to leave her lips as her cheeks got redder. She was mostly off him now. Only their legs remained touching. It was proving harder to separate their bodies from one another in the tight space of the cell. Miranda banged her head against the wall as she tried to stand. While her cell had been 10 feet by 10 feet, this one was barely over five feet in the direction she'd tried to roll. At this rate they would stay that way. Conjoined at the hip. Her hand slipped and her elbow slid into his stomach. He grunted.

"A little lower and you would have gotten the crown jewels," he said, a slight impish grin on his face. He propped himself up on his elbows to get a better look at her. It gave her the room to finally separate from him.

"Oh God, please forgive me!" she prayed. One of his eyebrows raised up just a hair higher than the other. Miranda crossed her arms.

"What are you doing on the floor, anyways? Wait. Don't tell me. You were tired." *Or tied up*, she thought. "Whatever. Get up. We need to get out of here and find the prince."

Eric obeyed by rising up from the floor.

"You know, for a figment of my imagination, you're pretty bossy." There was a long pause as he rubbed his chin. His gaze slid over her from head to toe. Miranda could feel her heart thumping louder in her chest. She didn't know that a look from Eric could give her those feelings.

" I like my women with bite," he whispered into her ear. Miranda tried to stare him down, but her eyes shifted away first. She was not about to dignify his disbelief in her existence with words or allow that comment to enter this... whatever their relationship was.

"You knew I would come for you if I could get out," she reminded him.

"Get out?" he said, questioning the last of her statement.

"Yes. Get out," she replied back. "It was easier than I thought it would be, actually. I kind of just, you know, went insane a little bit," she rambled. "Talking to the walls worked out. When was the last time you had anything to eat?" She took a breath to really look him over. Using her hands, she turned him left then right. He looked gaunt, as if the life had come out of his cheeks. All that healing must have really drained him.

"I can't remember," he told her. His voice was smooth. Her head drank up the words. She shook it to clear it. That taser must have been stronger than she realised. She still didn't know how long she'd been out. Eric must have been in the same boat.

He smiled that ambitious smile again.

"But that's why you're here, right?" he confirmed. "And Butterfly, I don't mind you being here one bit." He leaned into her, placing a hand on her. His eyes were ablaze in a way she'd only seen with her father when he stared at her mother. Miranda looked down at the hand he now had on her shoulder.

"I think that the lack of food and water has made you a little insane, too," she confirmed. She tried to shake him off, but she couldn't move. Her heart was racing too fast.

"You need food," she said forcing herself to turn away. She went to call up the drawer of food when she heard a small click.

She flung herself against one of the corners, willing herself to be invisible in the open white space. She was less than a foot from the door.

Whoever it was that opened the door did not come through it.

"All hail the mighty hero," a male voice boomed from the other side of the door. Eric ground his teeth.

"You call me a hero, yet you left me here to rot. So nice of you," Eric said.

"Well, you know how these things go," the man replied. "Capture a prince, ask for a large ransom, live happily ever after with

IMPERIAL EDGE 131

all my ill-gotten gains. Leave the prince to rot on a planet no one can get to."

"You are a disgrace," Eric spat at the man. The man must have ignored it because he didn't step into the room. He continued.

"Well, Your Highness. It seems that your empire cares nothing for you. It is a shame isn't it? To give one's life and to take the lives of others just to be another life to be taken." Miranda tried to hear what he said next, but her brain was stuck on what the guy called Eric. Prince. Eric wasn't the prince. The prince was the person Eric was sent to find and protect. She looked at the man in the cell again. He looked like Eric. His height, his face, the color of his hair, his uniform, the works. Everything was the same. Except his eyes. Yes, the color of his eyes was the same, but the glint in them. The fire. That was new. Eric had never had that fire.

Eric, who maybe wasn't Eric, shrugged. "What can I say? The people love me. The Empire? Maybe not so much."

"Their timeline is up. They haven't wired the payment for your release. Not that we were going to release you."

"So why bother a dead man?" Eric-who-wasn't-Eric said, his tone light; his expression playful.

"I wanted to see the expression on your face in person so I could remember for myself what hopelessness looks like." The man spat the words at Eric, punctuating each one. Arming them as weapons to strike his target. Eric-who-wasn't-Eric didn't even flinch. Didn't scream. He looked as nonchalant as ever. The exact opposite of what the guy expected to see, it seemed.

"This is goodbye," the man said. The panel slid back closed. Eric-who-wasn't-Eric slumped against the walls that were too tight. Miranda let out the breath that she had been holding.

"I thought for sure he was going to see you," he said, his head between his legs.

"Me, too," Miranda said, her voice catching on a dry throat.

'All the more reason to get out of here,' she thought.

She hadn't realized that it wasn't just the droids on this planet, but of course there would be rebels as well. Why would they take their prized possession to anything but a trap that they controlled? The stress of being surrounded and alone on an abandoned prison planet was getting to her.

"Okay, food and water. And then we're getting out of here," she told him.

"Glad my hallucination has a plan," Eric-who-wasn't-Eric said. "Not like I've tried to do both those things a thousand times already, but now that you're here it's all going to magically happen."

Miranda ignored the cutting words and beeped at the control panel, willing it to release its contents. One of the drawers to the left popped from the wall. Inside was the food capsules and two glasses of water.

"Great, enough for both of us," she said, handing Eric or His Highness or whoever this person was his capsules and glass. She really needed to get that cleared up. If this wasn't her Ironside, then she needed to know.

He took the glass from her and sniffed. Then he sipped its contents slowly. She couldn't tell if he was savoring it, or simply wary of his visions, handing him things to eat and drink. She quickly swallowed her own pellets and water.

"Who are you?" they both asked each other.

"I'm Miranda. Did you hit your head so hard in that crash that you forgot me?" she asked, placing her hand on his forehead.

"If you aren't Eric, who are you?" she asked. She wanted to verify, make sure that this was her Ironside. He had his face, but something was off in the eyes. They were different: colder, more sarcastic, more in control and somehow, just different, from her Ironside's eyes.

"Well, since you're a figment of my imagination, then for sure you know that I am Adam." He said, using his hands to add a flourish. "Or are you?" He handed the cup back to her. She placed it back in the drawer with her own, and then he rose to his feet to stand beside her.

"For a figment of my imagination, you sure are welcome sight," he said, running his hands through her hair and down her chin.

She froze at the touch. No man had ever touched her hair or face like that. An electric shock resonated through her. Sure, she had been around the boys in her family, been in wrestling games and hugging matches and pillow fights. Who didn't get into a good kickball match and not end up on top of one another? And, yeah, just a couple of seconds ago, she was hugging him, thinking that he was Eric, happy that he was alive. But suddenly, in that moment, every ounce of her body tensed, frozen under the pressure of this man's two fingers.

He tilted her up towards him and planted his lips down on hers. She blinked for a second, her brain reeling from the fact that this was her first kiss. That a prince of the empire had just stolen her first kiss. That she was in a jail cell sharing her first kiss with a prince. Her brain short circuited. She closed her eyes and reveled in the feeling of his lips on her.

They stood there that way, lips melding together. Then the absurdity of the situation hit her full force. It left an ache in her heart. She took both her hands and pushed back from him.

Stuttering she found the words to say, "What was that?" She was thankful that her mouth worked at all after all that. Prince Adam, Adamantium Hero of the Galaxium Wars, or whatever he was calling himself now, ran a finger over that perfect jaw of his as if shocked that his vision had substance.

He touched his lips and then reach for her again, as if wanting something that only she could provide. A dying man's daydream.

"We need to get out of her here," she said, turning back towards the door. "Do you think that they've gone?" Time was hard to tell in this place, but the talking and the kissing had to have been at least a few minutes. That must be enough time for the rebels to clear out. The guy had said he was leaving.

"Who knows?" She could feel the shrug in his words. He reached for her again, bending her head back towards him. His arms were like steel. His breath was hot on her skin. She turned her head just in time. The kiss landed on her cheek.

"If you are a prince, we're here to rescue you," she said.

"'We?'" he clarified. "I see only you." Miranda rolled her eyes. Was this how a war hero and a prince acted? Trapping women with kisses as those same women saved their lives. She turned to the control panel that popped out when she commanded the computer in Droid. Instead of asking the door to open, she pressed a button to unlock it. She didn't want to garner any attention, so she slowly slid it open. A good two or three inches, just enough to be able to look out and down the hall.

She looked both ways to make sure that it was clear. Then she slid it the rest of the way and motioned for him to follow her out the door.

'Which way did I come from?' she thought, looking backwards and forwards. She wanted to make sure that they weren't going to run into any more rebels or robot guards. In the end she chose right, hoping that that was the case.

"Stick behind me," she told him. He brushed up against her backside, then pressed the length of his body against hers and stopped.

"As close as glue," he said into her ear, just loud enough to be considered a whisper. Miranda's knees went weak. She registered that it wasn't from fear. The two of them headed down the hall Miranda in the front.

Never in her wildest nightmares had she imagined being on a mission to free a prince for a prison planet. She forced the thought down. She had to keep her mind in the moment. They rounded the next bend to find two robot guards standing at the end of the next hall guarding a cell. Miranda's breath caught. If they weren't careful, they would be joining whoever was in that cell.

Chapter 14

The robot guard was a dead giveaway. Miranda pulled back from the corner. Her mind filled in all the blanks. Adam ran straight into her, pushing her into the wall. Her first instinct was to push him off, then she remembered the droid.

"They must be keeping him in there," Miranda whispered to Adam. Adam nodded. She had already freed the prince; the only other living person that came to mind was Eric.

"Please, God; let it be Eric this time," she prayed. Adam looked at her expectantly. The army hero, winner of wars, prince of the galaxies, was looking at her for directions.

"We need a plan," she told him.

"So what is the plan," he said. She glared at him.

"Get their attention away from the cell and break the person out," Miranda replied. Adam nodded his not-Eric head up and down.

"And we are going to do that, how?" Adam asked.

"I don't know yet."

Just as the last word left her mouth, she turned her head back around the corner, coming face to face with the guards. A tentacle-like arm reached out to shock her. She stepped back and beeped.

"*Stop!*" she exclaimed in Droid. The droid stopped.

"Beep beep." *Turn around,* she said. It turned around. All of its old gears creaked as it twisted away.

"*Go patrol someplace else.*" Both droids started off down the hall away from the cell. Miranda heard a sigh. Adam was right up against her back.

Miranda beeped a little phrase at the wall. A control panel popped out. She pressed the sequence of buttons; that was becoming normal. The door slid open. She gestured at Adam to stay back. She didn't want them all to get captured or trapped if something happened to her on the other side. This might not be one of her crew waiting to be rescued. Adam got the message and slid back into the shadows.

The white walls greeted her. She was beginning to believe that they were some kind of hologram plastered over every cell to drive human beings insane. Within these planetary walls, even in its run down state, each of the rooms looked pristine. Yet she knew they couldn't have been dusted for years.

She looked over into the corner and jumped squeaking with fright. There on the ground was the remains of a human being. Tattered bits of clothing with bones; everything else rotted away a long time ago.

She felt the wind of an object swinging her direction. Out of the corner of her eye she saw an arm. She shifted to avoid it but she wasn't fast enough. She took the full force of the blow on her shoulders, just barely missing her head.

"Ouch," she yelled. "Is that what I get for trying to save you?"

The bone clanged to the ground, the Ironside that had been holding it shocked to find his teammate the one to open the door.

"I thought you were a rebel," the Ironside said as a way of apologising. Not Eric, but was Eric with him in the room? Then the truth registered.

"I can't believe you're alive," Miranda said. She looked at him with admiration. She didn't know if she could have survived a fall like that.

Behind the Iron side was the body of the other gunner, whose name she'd never learned.. She made the symbol for the dead, unable to get the words from her mouth. She had seen enough death today.

"Oh no. He's just sleeping." The Ironside kicked him. "Wake up, Axel."

Axel rubbed his eyes, knocking the sleep. Both he and the Ironside looked beat up; scratched uniforms and old healing bruises scarred them. But other than that, they looked relatively whole.

She shook her head. Happy reunions would have to wait. The rebels were all leaving; something big was happening. And they needed to get off planet. And back to the starship that brought them here before things blew up.

"Where is the pilot?" she asked. The Ironside and Axel shook their heads.

"Don't know, he got thrown from the ship when we fell."

"Beep, Beep," she said, opening the food drawer and allowing them both to have food and water to revive themselves. While the two of them gulfed down the pellets, she slid back the door enough to look out. Seeing that it was all clear she opened the regular door. She motioned Adam, she had to remind herself to call him Adam, to follow them down the left side. They hit an intersection and had to decide where to go from here.

So far all of the passages had just been rows and rows of prison cells. There was no direction to follow. No up or down, left or right that didn't equal more cells.

Miranda looked down both corridors and paused. The left corridor. Something about it looked odd. A blank wall of canvas where a cell should be, but wasn't. She whistled at the spot. Another control panel with a holo screen unfolded from the wall, its lights and circuits flashing to life.

She looked at the screen; everything was in Droid. All ones and zeros in ornate patterns flashing in a regular sequence in front of her. 'That's interesting,' she thought.

"What is that?" Axle asked, leaning over her left shoulder.

"Haven't you seen a console before?" she inquired of him. Axel shook his head.

"Can't say they have those on the ships I've been on," he said. "Most of the tech we get," he pointed at his head; there was a round disk right next to his left temple, "all the screens we interact with utilize these press points. Nothing requires audio interaction. And certainly not these." He looked down at the hard plastic buttons that made up the entrance keys to the command center station.

"Everything's holo. Not this," he said.

Miranda rolled her eyes. Of course, being from the army he would have knowledge of the newest tech. But her being from an outpost on a terraformed planetoid in the outer rings, all the technology on her planet, except for in the main cities, was at least 300 years old. New updated tech didn't reach colonial planets. Everything on her family farm had been voice command and push button operated. Even Oscar.

"This," she explained to him, "is a control panel. This will show us," she moved her finger up to the screen, "where we're at, and possibly a map of where we need to get to."

"Where do we need to get to the next?" asked Adam. He'd stuck his head over her other shoulder. Miranda looked from Axle to Adam and then hung her head in disgust.

"See this here. That's where we are at now." She pointed up into the left corner of the screen with its flashing ones and zeros. "This down here," she pointed to the other side of the screen, "is the launching bay."

"These here," she marked out different points, "are the gateway entrances that will get us from where we're at to the launching bay." She typed a couple of things into the keys. It took a moment for the computer to register. But then an area to the left started to click. A piece of paper spit out from the machine.

Axel jumped back in surprise when the thing touched his leg.

"Get off! Get off!" he screamed. Miranda gave him a look.

"It's just paper," she said, retrieving the slip. The gunner was hunkering behind Adam, fear screaming from his eyes.

"Haven't you seen paper before?" she said. He straightened and tried to look tough. But Miranda would never see him that way again. He would forever be the man afraid of paper printouts.

"We need to hurry," she said to suppress her smile. "These halls might have guards."

Miranda remembered. It wasn't just the robot guards they had to worry about. Somewhere in this prison, rebels roamed. If they found them before they could secure blasters, they would be dead.

"Who put you in the cell, anyway?" she asked, typing away on the computer, trying to get more information out of it. Little white pieces of paper poured out the side every couple of minutes.

"Don't know," Axel shrugged. "Woke up in there with the Ironside. You'd be better off to ask him."

"Robert. My name is Robert," said the Ironside. They all looked at him blankly. "But everyone calls me Fox." He dropped his head down and looked at the floor.

"So you don't mind if that's what we call you then?" Miranda asked.

"No," he said. "Fox is fine." He hissed the last word through his teeth. He took off his helmet to tussle his hair. It was the first time Miranda had ever seen him without it. It kind of took the edge off, made him go from being a piece of equipment to an actual human being. For some reason she was expecting him to look like Eric; that somehow becoming an Ironside made you look like a handsome jerk. But no, his features were very different from both Adam's and Eric's face. His hair, for one, was blond. It fell limp around his round face. The roots were black against his sun bleached skin. His eyes were a deep brown and shaped like brush strokes that carved out calligraphy letters.

Miranda blinked. She paused, waiting for him to continue. He didn't.

"So Robert, how did you guys end up in the cell?" she asked.

He shook his head.

"We fell back. The ship separated and we fell back onto a ledge on one of the lower docks. We would have kept falling if we hadn't caught on it." He paused; his brow creased in thought. "Don't know how long we were there. Couldn't move, being strapped in. Didn't know how stable it was if I unstrapped. Three droids came down from above. Hovered in the air and then opened fire. I couldn't get out of my harness in time before the things shot. I thought for sure we were dead." He stopped talking, not wanting to remember what waking up from death feels like.

"Go on," Miranda encouraged him. She needed as many details as possible if she was going to have a chance of forming a plan or finding Eric.

"When I woke up in that cell... It must have been some kind of stunner. I knew we were still alive because I was still in my suit. And the tech was still operational. If partially damaged from the fall."

Miranda nodded, continuing her search on the computer. Now that she had a clear path to the landing bay, she was searching just in case. Just in case Eric had survived too.

Axel whistled. "Must be some stunners if they get through Ironside armor."

"I found him," Miranda said, cutting off what Axel was going to say next.

"Found who?" Adam asked, looking at her screen of ones and zeros, not able to read any of her printouts.

"Eric."

Adam looked at her, trying to understand what she was saying.

"Our leader, the other Ironside we came with. I found him."

There was a clicking sound from down the hallway.

"Time to go," she said. She grabbed the stack of papers out of Axel's hands and made a left turn down the hallway, away from the noise.

The rest of the group filed in behind. She had a plan. She had a map, she was going to find Eric, and then they were going to get off this rock with the prince, just like he had wanted from the very beginning.

Chapter 15

"Here's the deal," Miranda said. "This is the hangar where they're keeping active shuttles. When I made this recording, it showed only one operational shuttle. That's the good news." She pointed to some of the ones and zeros on one of her pieces of paper, hoping that the outline of symbols meant as much to them as it did to her. Adam looked on in interest. Axel still wanted to put distance between him and this paper stuff, just in case maybe it exploded. Miranda didn't let it slow her down.

"Now, what I know for sure, is that this entire area has the largest concentration of humans on this planet, to include Eric. He's being kept on the shuttle. That's the bad news. Most likely," and she tried to emphasize this point, "it is the last shuttle, and our only option for getting off this rock."

Adam sighed.

"That leaves us with our second problem," she said.

"Our second problem?" Adam asked. Miranda nodded.

"They have weapons," she stated. The three others looked from each other and back to her. "I'm assuming that all of your weapons were taken," she added to be helpful. The Ironside hung his head. Adam shrugged his shoulders and the gunner scratched the back of his head.

"My weapon was attached to the vehicle," Axel said. "If you want I can go see if they are still there."

"No thanks," Miranda said. Most gunners weren't issued a private weapon. They were just put in front of whatever gun was in the shuttle or ship that they were being transported in.

"Adam, of course, being a captured prisoner, you had your weapons stripped before arriving on planet," Miranda said. She turned to Fox. "That leaves you, since I didn't have any on this mission to begin with." She looked expectantly at the Ironside. The poor guy shook his head.

"Droids knocked us out after the fall. They must have stripped me clean. All I've got is my tech gear," He said.

Miranda nodded, accepting all this.

"If we're going to have any chance against the rebels, we need weapons," she said. They agreed. She flipped through her paper until she got to another page. "I printed this out."

All three of them looked expectantly at her since they couldn't read what was on the page. "This is where the armory is," she said, pointing to a box. "That is where we're going next."

"I'm ready to blow this joint," Axel said. Adam gave him a look. "What?"

Miranda headed off down the hallway.

"Be quiet, stay alert," she said. "And let's make it out of here." She didn't know when she became the go-to leader, but without Eric, somehow she felt like it was her responsibility to get these guys home.

The planet twisted and turned around them in left and rights. It was meant to be a maze. Every once in a while, they would have to flatten themselves against a wall because of a droid. But they hadn't seen a rebel soldier yet.

'Whoever that guy is who talked to Adam back at the cell,' Miranda thought, 'certainly got it right. They've already left planet, or are in the middle of leaving planet, leaving all of these prisoners to rot in an area of space that has been left for that very purpose by the Galactic Empire.'

As time stretched, Miranda wondered how many of these places were still floating around, left to their own devices, abandoned and useless. Leaving their prisoners to rot to death.

She found the door to the armory. It looked like any of the other doors. If she hadn't had her map, she wouldn't have been able to tell the difference between it and any of the cells that they had passed long since.

"Here we are," she whispered to the boys while pointing towards the door. They slumped over; one to the left, looking down the hall, and one to the right as she whistled necessary beeps for the control panel and typed in the sequence to open the door. She was getting pretty good at this. It might have been old tech, but hey, it was at least something she was useful at. The door slid open and Adam stepped inside. The room was near bare. A single backpack, a helmet, the odd laser pack or two, three short-range blasters on the far wall, and a single cannon that could cut the whole side off a shuttleship hanging above them. The rest was empty. There where shelves for everything a normal imperial armory should have, just with nothing in them.

Adam took very little time to pull everything off the racks, strapping different things to his back, testing each of the weapons to make sure that they were chargeable or could hold the necessary charge.

He then proceeded to bring things out. He handed a single blaster to Miranda, the cannon blaster, and a side blaster to Axel. To the other Ironside he handed the third blaster. He kept a small pack and a laser sword and some sort of backpack gun that Miranda had never seen and might be older tech than even her planet kept.

"It's like someone knew just what we needed and left it here for us," he said to her. "It's old, but it's still good."

"This stuff is classic!" Axel said, his mouth gaping.

"Let's just hope it fires accurately after all these years," said Fox. He let the gun warm up under his fingers. The bright orange lights pulsed across the barrel.

Miranda nodded. At least now they were armed and had the ability to go after Eric.

"Hanger's five floors up and over," she told her crew. Adam took the lead. She took up the middle. Axel and Fox were at the rear with their guns at the ready. It was almost as if they were in an

Ironside sandwich given the fact Adam was an Ironside, even if he wasn't in full uniform.

As they approached the hangar the lighting seemed to get brighter, as if closer to the top of the planet, the more the sun penetrated through the corridors and cracks. Miranda used her blaster to shield her eyes. Not the best move, but the gun seemed to do the trick. Better than putting it down, she reasoned.

"I would just like to know who built this place," Axel complained. "Must have been a bunch of idiots not to put any labels on anything."

'Or geniuses to hide them all where human prisoners couldn't find them,' Miranda thought.

"Keep moving," Fox barked. "I'm getting an off feeling about this place."

Miranda rolled her eyes. They were in the corridors of an abandoned prison; of course he was getting a bad feeling.

Adam raised his hand, bringing them all to a stop. He motioned them to get their backs up against the wall.

The first shot whizzed past Miranda's head, barely missing her. Her eyes followed it in slow motion. The green light made a blast mark on the back of the wall where her head had been. Another shot passed by her ear. She could feel the heat of it redden her face.

Miranda's legs melted from beneath her. The two Ironsides positioned themselves on either side of the door. Careful to aim, shoot, pullback, aim, shoot, pullback, rotating back and forth between the two of them. Miranda watched everything as if the world had turned to water with her legs.

"They don't have any big guns," Axel pointed out from his position on the left. Adam nodded. "You ok?" Axel said above her. Miranda nodded, unable to understand the words. Everything was so slow. Axel crouched next to Miranda. He put a hand on her shoulder and shook her gently. His gun was in the other hand, ready to fire if needed.

"Just breathe," he said.

"Breathe," she repeated.

"Axel, you're up," Adam announced. Axel nodded his head once, slung his gun around the corner and blasted away. Boom, boom, boom, boom.

The heavy rain of fire shook Miranda to her bones. She didn't know how Axel could handle all that pressure. Her ears were ringing and she wasn't the one firing the thing. It was hard enough being behind him. She couldn't imagine what it was like in front of him.

Adam made the motion to move forward. Axel kept up his suppressive fire. Miranda got back up into her Ironside sandwich. She got her gun out, pushed the safety off and put it up in a firing pose just in case.

Shots rang out around her. But the Ironsides held up their suppressive fire while moving from one stack of cargo to the next. It kept the rebels' shots wide or out of range.

Miranda crouched behind another load of covered cargo. The landing bay was littered with them. It was making it easy to duck, hide, and weave their way to the shuttle craft.

Pew pew. The sound of laser fire created a melody of its own around her, reminding her of the danger. If any of those shots landed that would be it. She would be dead.

The hanger was marred black with different pockmarks. Each a reminder of what was really happening. They were in a fight for their lives. And if they didn't make it to that ship... Miranda put the thought out of her mind.

Laser blasts sizzled past. Adam signed for them to move forward again. Miranda forced her legs to stand up and move. She was not going to die here. There was a body sprawled on the floor. She had to roll over the top of it or be tripped into the line of fire. The smell of cooked meat hit her nose. Vomit rose in her throat. She held it back. They might have been rebels, but they were still people. And if she let it get to her right now she'd end up just like them.

As they passed another set of crates she noticed a smoking set of gray-black trousers with tons of pockets. She wished that her uniform had pockets like that. Maybe that was the best thing about being a rebel. They could wear cargo pants to hold all their stuff.

IMPERIAL EDGE

A blast missed her head by inches. The heat of it sizzled her cheek. Mirand ducked down just in time to see two rebels run for the ship's gangplank. It rose into the air. The rest of her team was too busy trying to suppress the fire to notice their only way off this rock lifting off.

"They are going to get away without us," Miranda screamed over the noise. There was no sign that Adam or Fox had heard her. They kept moving forward, ducking behind empty cargo crates. Trying to make a hole towards the ship. Two rebels were using the ship's gangplank to hold them back. Miranda could feel the cold burn from the flight engines gearing up for take-off.

Miranda stomped her foot and screamed, "They are getting away!" Adam yanked her to the ground, a blaster bolt singeing the top of her head. Fox shot back, knocking the rebel off the plank.

"Get your gun up and be ready," Adam said, shoving her blaster into her chest.

Miranda sat there stunned. She'd just almost died. If Adam hadn't pushed her out of the way, she would be another smoking corpse filling this place.

The gangplank floated above their heads now. The ship made a one eighty in the air as the last of the rebels cleared back from the closing door. Adam swore. Miranda felt like doing much the same. The ship door closed all the way out of reach. Axel fired some of his cannon shots, but nothing landed. The hull of the ship meant to protect from the dangers of space, the hand cannon doing nothing to its shell.

They all watched the ship rise higher and higher away from them.

"Too late," Fox said. "We were too..." His last word was cut off by a boom. A wave of energy from the explosion washed over them, knocking Fox to the ground. It pushed Miranda back off her feet. She felt her head collide with the edge of a cargo crate. Her eyes teared up and everything went fuzzy.

Chapter 16

"What in the Empire's long reach just happened?" Axel asked. He'd been the farthest back, laying down suppressing fire with his cannon of a gun so the wave had missed him.

"It blew up," Adam said. He was on the ground like the rest of them. Just sitting there. His body thrown back into the pile of crates he'd been maneuvering around when it happened. The imprint of his suit pressed into the wood. In as much shock as everyone else. He sat there unmoving, the words coming out, but nothing with them. "It just blew up."

Miranda wanted to say something, anything to make it better. But it wasn't better. The ship, their way off world, had exploded right before their eyes. She couldn't piece the puzzle together. It made no sense. They had gotten away. Were ready to push off world. There was no reason for it to have exploded.

"Fox, report," Adam said. The poor Ironside lay face first in the dirt. He tried to speak but the ground absorbed the words. He tried to roll over, only to get stuck halfway on his side.

"System armour still operational, but its malfunctioning. Shrapnel penetration in the back panel and right leg." There was a long pause as he moved his leg testing its functionality. "Nothing penetrated the arm, but I won't be space walking in this suit any time soon," Fox said.

Adam nodded. "Axel."

"All charge packs are used up," Axel said. "Might be something we can scrape together from here, but it looks like the rebels took everything with them. Probably added to the boom."

Adam nodded again. "Miranda?"

It was less of an order and more of a question. Was he actually worried about her? She looked into his masked eyes and winced. Two of him swam in and out of her vision. She tried to stand but she couldn't find the ground.

"Miranda?" he asked again, some urgency in his tone.

"She's been hit," Axel provided for her. She wanted to tell them she was fine. That it was the impact with the crate and not anything else. That the world was just spinning, but if that they gave her enough time, she really would be fine, but no words came from her mouth.

"We need to get her to a med bay," Axel said. The two Adams in front of her nodded in agreement.

"The only med bay is up on the ship," Fox pointed out.

"And the only way to the ship just blew up in front of us," Adam added.

"Either I got off a very lucky shot..." Axel reasoned.

"Or their own people rigged it to blow," Fox finished for him.

"All great questions," Adam said, "that don't help. Facts: our ride is shot and the only person that can communicate with the computer systems here is in need of medical care."

That's when she heard it. A faint beeping sound of a Type One Droid. At first she thought it was just the ringing in her ears. But no. This was a beep boop that she'd heard far too many times before to ever confuse it with a concussion.

"Oscar!" Miranda cried. The little droid rolled into her line of vision. She'd never been so happy to see him in her entire life.

"Beep beep boop," he scolded her.

"Yes, I know," she tried to say back, but the words came out slow and slurred. The little droid rolled up to her head and stuck out a tentacle-like arm. There were two of them in Miranda's vision, but she couldn't trust that. She couldn't trust anything she was seeing at the moment. An arm touched her head. The thought that she'd never seen anything close to arms on the droid entered her mind and just as quickly left it.

She felt a small prick at the side of her head. It hurt, but nothing compared to the pain she was already in.

"What's the droid doing to her," Axel asked.

"I think," Adam started to say, then stopped. Miranda opened her eyes and looked up at him. He was one person now. Fuzzy around the edges, but still there was only one of him in her line of site.

"I think he's stabilizing her," Adam finished.

"I've never seen anything like it," Fox said from somewhere to her right. She didn't try to move her head around to see what he was looking at. It still hurt too much. She tried to talk again.

"I'm ok," she said. The words actually came out and didn't sound like they were underwater. Adam reached out and put a hand on her shoulder.

"Just let the droid do whatever it's doing," he said. Miranda shrugged. Her shoulders responded to her request. She could feel her fingers and toes again. That was nice.

Oscar's one tentacle arm retreated back to wherever it had come from and Miranda stood up.

"I'm fine," she said patting down each of her arms and legs banishing the tingles and hurts from her fall. Adam nodded at her slowly.

"We're in a jam," Adam said. "We can't call the ship, even if we wanted to. I'm afraid that the rebels may have taken it over. If that's the case..."

"Then they'd ignore us and leave us here to rot anyway," Fox finished. Miranda nodded to show she was listening.

"You said it yourself, that was the last shuttle off this rock," Axel supplied.

"Yes," Miranda agreed.

"So even if it hadn't had Eric on it," Adam added. There was a flash of anger in his eyes, but then it was gone. "We would still have needed it to get up to the ship."

"So we might have survived the exposition," Fox said.

"But if we don't get up to the ship before it leaves, " Adam continued.

"We're dead," Axel added for comfort.

"Ok, I get it," Miranda said.

"Beep Bop Boop," Oscar chimed in.

"Not now Oscar. I'm trying to think," she said to the droid.

"Beep bop boop," he said again.

"I get that you know, but we are trying to think of a way off this rock and unless you know where that may be then we got nothing," Miranda said.

The little droid pulled on her pants, pushing her to and fro. He wanted her to follow him.

"Fine," she said, giving in. Her head wasn't one hundred percent yet anyway and all the talking and thinking gave her a headache.

"We're playing follow the droid," she told the others. Axel looked at Fox, Fox looked at Adam, Adam shrugged and followed after Miranda, who was already wobbling after the droid.

They passed through a long hallway devoid of anything, into another hangar bay. It was as big as the last one. There were scattered boxes here and there; otherwise it was empty. It took some time to weave in and out of the boxes. At the middle of the room the droid stopped.

"Beep beep," he said bumping the large crate in front of him. Miranda looked from the crate to the droid and back again.

"I can't believe it," she said.

"Beep boop," the droid answered. Adam, Fox, and Axel caught up behind her.

"We have a way off this rock," she said pointing at the crate.

"But..." Adam said.

"It will only fit two, max," she said. Every face fell. There were four of them. How were they ever to choose who would go and who would be left behind?

"I'm staying," Axel said at the same time Miranda said, "and there's another catch,"

"What's the second catch," Fox asked. Miranda took in a long breath.

"This is a H176 planetary escape pod," she said. Oscar shocked the crate. Planks fell back to reveal a small pod that looked to be a little taller and just a bit wider than Adam in full dress uniform.

"Oh," the three soldiers said together.

IMPERIAL EDGE

"That means?" Adam asked.

"That means that unless someone else on this team knows Droid, I've got to be the one driving it." All three men looked at her.

The pod ship was pretty cool for being over two hundred years old. The lines were a bright metallic shade, something between vibranium and silver, while the outer shell shown white that changed depending on what angle you looked at it. The ship reminded her of an Easter Egg wrapped in wires and ready to be dipped into different colors. It was a common practice to celebrate the union of God back in the Eternal place.

"But Fox is our best shot at saving the ship," Axel pointed out.

"And Adam is our mission," Fox said. "Rescuing him is a top priority."

Miranda sighed. "So you see the problem."

"I'll stay," Adam offered. "If you can't take the ship back then we're dead anyways. If you do take the ship back then I know you'll send a shuttle to pick us back up."

"No," Axel and Fox said at the same time. The two men looked at each other, wondering which would be the first to say more. Axel ducked his head and crossed his arms.

"No," Fox said again, "You are the mission. What if we get up there and the ship's already gone?"

"I could set the pod up to signal a rescue, but…" Miranda let the word hang between the three of them.

"No," Axel said again. "I ain't gonna be the guy that messed up the mission." At the same time Fox said, "Mission first." The two of them looked at each other then looked away. It was decided then.

Miranda stepped into the pod and started it up. Her fingers danced over the keys she knew all too well from all the practice she'd gotten opening doors in this place. It would be a tight fit. The two of them in a pod made for one. She would have to sit on his lap. The thought of being that close to an Ironside, let alone the crown prince, brought heat to her cheeks. She never believed she would see royalty in her lifetime. The royal professionals never made their way out into the territories. Now she'd saved him from a cell and was going to be riding with him, her back against his front all the way to the spaceship. It was too much for her heart. She ducked her head behind the control panel to hide her embarrassment.

"Ship's all warmed up," she said.

Adam slipped in behind her. She rested her weight against him.

"Beep boop," Oscar chided.

"No, I haven't forgotten about you," Miranda responded back. She leaned over half in half out of the craft to get a good handle on the droid. Then she lifted him up onto her lap. He made it harder to reach the controls, but he fit.

"Sorry," she said, realizing that she'd just stuck her butt in the crown prince's face.

"It's fine," he said, "let's just get out of here." His voice had lowered. She couldn't see his face, but something in her wanted to. Wanted to know what he was really thinking in that moment. But she settled on closing the hatch and starting the launch sequence.

Adam had placed the blasters in such a way that the stocks hung over his lap a bit. It was the only way they'd fit in the pod, but it meant they were constantly poking Miranda. It made for a very uncomfortable seat. Not that she expected this ride to be comfortable, but since they were traveling to their possible doom she wanted to be as fresh as could be. She shifted back and forth, trying to find a spot that didn't pinch without disposing Oscar from her lap.

"Miranda," Adam growled. She started, half sitting up and banging her knees. He knew her name. She hadn't even remembered telling it to him. But he knew it well enough to call her by it.

"Do you mind?" he asked.

"Sorry," she said, settling back into him. She stopped squirming even though the position was as uncomfortable as it had been before. She was just going to have to be pinched.

There was a large jerk. All three of them were pressed forward, then back in a sudden motion. The spacecraft had taken off.

"Here goes nothing," Miranda said, pressing the last button in the sequence. She closed her eyes and whistled the starter command. The ship broke through the planet's upper atmosphere and everything in the cabin went weightless. They were packed in so tightly nothing really moved, but Miranda still felt better given that all her weight wasn't pressing her down onto the hard blasters.

"How long until we reach the ship?" Adam asked. Miranda whistled a few commands.

"About half an hour," she said, reading the zeros and ones on the screen. They fell silent again.

"Since we're stuck like this, why don't you tell me about how you got into this mess in the first place." she said. Miranda felt his breath on the back of her neck, her hair having decided to fly up into the space above her ears.

"I was a fool," he said.

"I doubt that," Miranda said. The man she had met and rescued was anything but a fool. No, something else had happened.

"I was meeting with some rebel members," he started his tale. "We'd been fighting their forces on an outpost planet near Reverie 14. It's in the guardian cluster near outer territories. It had been a tough two weeks. I'd thought that their side was as tired of fighting as ours. They had more losses, but my men were done. They just wanted for it to all be over so they could go home and kiss their loved ones."

Miranda thought of her loved ones. Her heart ached to see all of them again, just once. She felt she knew how those soldiers did.

"So when the rebel leader offered a truce to talk about a surrender," Adam continued after a moment, "I jumped at the chance. It was at a secure location between both of our territories. Watchable by both sides. So I never saw it coming." Adam paused to collect his thoughts. Miranda was glued to the story. They had nothing better to do and it was proving interesting.

"Go on," she encouraged him.

"It was a trap, the whole thing from the very beginning. A trap to get me. The men I brought with me, they were good lads, most of them, but the regular army sent backups. I didn't know any of them. That should have been my first clue, but I was so intent on brokering peace and getting home by Easter that I failed to take the proper precautions." He stopped talking and laid his head against her back between her shoulder blades. He rested it there, breathing against her neck. They stayed that way for quite a while. Him resting on her. Her sitting on the edge of her seat, waiting for him to continue before he noticed how red her face was flushing.

"And?" she coaxed him.

"They struck from all sides. All the soldiers were rebels in disguise. The two Ironsides I brought with me didn't have a chance. I was captured, but not before I took out a number of them first," he added.

Miranda giggled. Of course he would emphasize that part of the story. Men always did. When this was all over the stories would grow from five to twenty to one hundred and beyond. That's just what happened. Like her father's trout stories.

"I fail to see the humor," Adam scolded. They fell silent again.

"We're here," she said at last. His tale had taken up the whole space ride. Miranda held her breath. The holo screen in front of her turned black as the pod slipped into the shadow cast by the interstellar ship. Something bumped against their pod. A whining sound echoed as the thing scraped across the bottom of the pod.

Kuthunck.

Another something hit the top of the craft. They were still on course for the landing bay, but something was wrong. Very wrong. Miranda just didn't know what.

"What was that?" Adam whispered in her ear.

Luck must have been on their side because the landing bay's door were wide open. Black shapes, dots in the ink really, littered the path between them and the landing bay. Miranda's mind refused to process it.

They were running on silent. No reason to give the rebels they knew were waiting for them any reason to think that they were there. She watched as the landing bay doors began to close. She had one of two options, speed up towards them, coming in hot and possibly being detected because of the noise, or hack the computer system from the pod's remote port and have the landing bay doors reopen, which could also draw the attention of the rebels.

Miranda hit the excelerator. The ship lurched forward. The closer they got to the bay door, the fewer things they hit. Whatever had been spaced was traveling out.

The doors were picking up speed as they came closer to the opening. Miranda crossed her fingers and hit the excelerator button again. If they didn't pick up speed they weren't going to make it. The doors were closing too fast. The pod was too committed to its course. Either they were going to just make it or they were going to be splat balls against the side of the ship.

They passed through the opening as the doors slid shut behind them, locking them in. Miranda didn't sigh with relief just yet/ they were going the pod's maximum speed straight at the dock walls. She hit the left turn button hard, sending them into a tailspin.

Around and around they went hovering above the landing zone, but it was just enough to slow them down and get them to stop.

Miranda dumped Oscar to the floor and threw up. Adam reached behind her just as he exited the ship. The motion of the landing left her head spinning and her body wrenching.

"Bee boop boo," Oscar said, pulling at Miranda's shirt. She put her hand to her head.

"What's he trying to tell us?" Adam asked. He'd recovered enough to be able to put his hands on his knees.

"Rebels are coming, we have less than a minute," she said between gasps of air. Miranda scanned the bay. There was nothing to hide behind. Everything in the hangar had been spaced.

"Beep boop boop!" the little droid cried.

"I know, I just don't know," Miranda yelled back. The little droid pointed at a spot on the wall.

"Over here," Miranda said, dragging Adam to the wall with her. Oscar stuck his tentacle arm into the wall. A panel popped free, revealing a maintenance shoot.

Oscar lost no time in climbing in. Miranda followed.

"Come on," she waved at Adam to get in behind her. He'd stopped at the door.

"With the ship landing they'll be expecting someone. That someone has to be me." His eyes gleamed with determination and something else, fear maybe? But he was the scourge of the galaxies. He couldn't possibly be afraid.

"Get in here," she said reaching for him. He stepped to the side.

"You're our only shot," he said.

"No," Miranda protested.

"Save me," Adam said, closing the panel door behind him.

Miranda stood up to the grate, not knowing what to do. She heard a door slide open, then footsteps. Adam had somehow run back to the ship. Miranda watched watched through the grate as two rebels leveled guns at her prince.

"Well, well; lookie what escaped his prison cell after all," said a female rebel. She had bright red hair that shone crimson in the bay lights. Her face was heart shaped, her eyes a beautiful green color of a field in full bloom. She was fit. Her blaster hung off a hook belt that rested at an angle off her hip. She wore a light brown, natural-fiber shirt over a dark brown pair of leggings that showed off her legs. The picture perfect poster girl for rebel causes. The other one spat.

"Better for him if he'd stayed down there to die," the male rebel said. He was a head taller than the girl, with broad shoulders and a square face. A brown mop of hair poked out around the edges of a blue pilot cap. It was a size too small, so it had to be borrowed, or stolen off a newly made corpse. Miranda grimaced at the thought.

He lifted up his blaster as if to fire point blank at Adam. The woman put a hand on top of the gun and pushed it down.

"Not so hasty, buddy," she said. "Captain might want him alive." Miranda's heart skipped a beat. Was the captain of the ship really a rebel spy? Had he given them all up to steal his own ship? The possibilities made her head hurt more than their landing had.

"Whatever you say, love," he cooed back. It didn't take much to determine who the brains were and who was the brawn in this team.

"What are you doing here?" Adam asked ask them as the girl tied him up.

"We'd come to see if there were any hangers on," the male said.

"What about your ship?" Adam said. The two exchanged looks and then broke out into laughter. Mirand heard the slip click of the restraints sizing to Adam's wrists.

"Move," the girl said. She pushed him forward with the tip of her own gun. Adam stumbled forward, gained his footing and then started walking forward of his own free will. His shoulders were back, his head high like he was their leader and they were the ones captured.

"So you weren't here for the last shuttle?" he asked again.

"You talk too much, pretty boy," the guy said. He swung his gun out, hitting Adam in the back of his head as he passed the man. Adam dropped like a rock.

"Look what you've done now," the girl complained.

The man shrugged.

"He was walking of his own free will and you went and knocked him out," she said.

He scratched under his cap.

"Well, I ain't carrying him three flights of stairs all the way to the bridge lift," she spat at him.

He looked at her then at the body.

"You dropped him, you carry him," she said.

"Nah," he said.

Her green eyes flashed as her hand hit the back of his head in and upward sweep. It knocked his hat from his head.

"Ouch," he said, rubbing his head.

"I'm telling the boss you left the prince unattended in the landing bay," she said, stepping over Adam as she walked towards the door. The big guy bent over and picked up his hat. He looked at her, then at the prince, then back at her as the door closed behind her. He brushed the hat off and sighed. Then he slung Adam over his shoulder with one hand and headed out of the landing bay.

Miranda turned away from the grate. Her breaths came hard. Her mind refused to let go of the words the two rebels had said as she climbed up the shaft after Ozcar.

They hadn't been waiting for their people at all. The landing bay had been open for another reason. They knew the last rebel shuttle wasn't coming and they were ok with that. Planned it, even.

Worse, they'd opened those doors to space. They said they were checking for hangers on. That had only one possibility. They had been spacing the crew!

A shudder ran through Miranda's body. Her grip on the service ladder faltered. She flailed mid air for a minute before regaining her hold. Her heart thundered in her chest. Oscar turned back to look at her, then carried on. What kind of monster locked the crew in a landing bay and then opened it up to space, then watched and waited for all of them to die?

'Rebels,' her mind told her back.

They had reached the top of the shaft. Two went off in each direction. One towards the bridge, the other towards the engine room. She had to think. Adam was relying on her to save him. She'd already failed Eric, the crew, Axel, Fox, and her family. She was not going to let their sacrifices be in vain.

"Think, Miranda, think," she whispered to herself. Oscar made a low single beep.

"I know, I just..." Then a thought hit her. There was a way to save Adam. To incapacitate the rebels without killing Adam. The answer sat right in front of her. She signaled Oscar over to her.

"Beep, beep." *Take the panel off,* she told him. He reached out with this tentacle arm and removed the panel, exposing the internal wires of the ship's main operating system.

"Beep, beep, beep." She gave Oscar his orders. Excited by the adventure, the little droid scurried down the corridor to the right. Miranda took the left down the corridor towards the bridge. They'd called him 'captain,' so that's the only place he would be. She looked down at her band. Oscar had told her how long it would take for him to hack the system. She'd set her band to that exact number. Now all she had to do was get into place and watch until it happened. Easy, she told herself. If only it was as easy as she thought it would be.

Chapter 17

The duct got tighter the closer she got to the bridge. One would think that with regulation interstellar builds like this one, the ship would have straight, even passageways that mirrored the decks below. That was not the case. These tunnels felt more like an afterthought. Something the builders had connected up out of necessity at the last minute. It made for sharp turns and less than ideal corners for crawling on one's hands and knees.

Every so many feet she would stop and look through a vent, being careful not to be scene by a passing rebel. She needed to stop by the bridge; no farther. Luckily for her the passages were stable. Nothing creaked as she moved. At least she was thankful for that.

She looked through the vent into a round room. This one was different. She passed a row of personal cabins, all empty. Then she saw a couple of converse rooms, all deserted. The very next set of vents looked out over a wide, round room with multiple chairs all facing a large screen. There were people in this room. She went to the next vent to see if she could get a better view. Two bright blues eyes stared directly back at her. She covered her mouth to keep from screaming. Maybe the man hadn't seen her. Maybe he wouldn't say anything. She stared back at him, willing him to not see her. After she didn't hear him cry out she allowed herself to look him over. His dress uniform showed that he was a high ranking officer. Miranda looked at his face again. The blues eyes still stared right at her, unblinking. She looked down at her timer. It had been over a minute and the man hadn't blinked.

Realization dawned in her eyes. This man, the man that had warned them about the planet, the one that had kept them in quarantine. The one she remembered as the Captain of the ship, was dead in front of her. She'd been too late to save him.

She forced herself to move past him to the next grate. She needed a better view, and he was blocking this one.

The next grate opened up right beyond the captain's chair. Miranda could see the room up close now. Adam sat on his knees in front of a man in the captain's chair. All she could see of him was his hair which was mostly covered by a large ornate hat. Most likely the captain's hat with all its gold decorations.

He had a gun on his knee, the barrel sticking out past the edge of the chair. On the floor in front of Adam lay another bound Ironside. His helmet was off, exposing his strong chin and dimpled face. It was Eric. Miranda's heart skipped a beat. He was alive. Eric was alive.

She'd been so sure that he was on that shuttle, the one that the rebels blew up. Here he was. Unconscious, but alive.

Adam's lips moved. He was talking. Miranda strained to hear his words.

"You won't get away with this," Adam said.

"But you royal pain in my butt, I already have," the man said. His voice sounded familiar, but Miranda couldn't place it.

"Now all that's left is seeing you properly dead, but not before I blast this one back to where he belongs." The wannabe captain raised the gun, leveling it on Eric.

"Stop!" Miranda cried. Her voice echoed out of the air vent and down into the bridge. Everyone froze.

"Who was that?" the man in the chair said to the other rebels on deck. The redhead from earlier was the first to respond.

"It sounded like it came from the vent," she said. The big guy she was with whipped out his blaster and started to fire at the vents. Miranda ducked back out of the way of the fire.

"Are you crazy?" she heard the captain rebel say. The fire stopped.

"Luce, be a dear and go catch the mouse in the walls," he said. Miranda huffed. She was no mouse. The least he could do was call her a dog, or maybe a rat. Not a mouse. Miranda took one last look at her band. Four more minutes to go. She was too early, but if she hadn't said anything then she would have been too late to save Eric. She wasn't going to let that happen again. Not today; not ever.

"I caught something." The redhead waved her out with a gun. "Come on mousy, the cat needs to have some fun." Miranda put her hands up above her head and followed the woman out onto the bridge.

"Well, well, well, look that we got here," the man in the captain's chair said. He swiveled the chair around to face her. There, sitting in the captain's seat, was none other than their dead pilot Rycer. Who was very much alive and killing people.

"Rycer," Miranda breathed.

"That's Captain Rycer now to you," he said. "That goes for all of you." He swung his chair around and gave Adam's face a pinch.

"Isn't that how it goes," he taunted. His voice was low and full of menace as he said, "Whoever kills the king gets to wear the crown." Adam looked up at Rycer, murder radiating from his eyes.

"Or in this case, the captain's hat," Rycer said. He tapped the hat on his head, as if that's all that mattered.

"Back to the matter at hand," he said turning to face her. "How ever did you get here?" The redhead pushed her blaster into Miranda's ribs. Pain shot through her side from where it impacted with her flesh.

Miranda stepped forward.

"The captain asked you a question," the redhead said. She fixed Miranda in her blaster sights. Miranda could smell the soot from the barrel.

"What is this, a 'kill me if I don't talk' setup?" Miranda joked. They all stared at her. She'd gotten herself into the mess and she could get herself out of it. All she needed was time.

"I have a question for you," Miranda shot back.

"The little mouse has a question for our Captain," the brute said. Now his too small cap made sense. It was the first mate's cap. He'd probably taken it off the guy before they spaced the crew. He was mimicking Rycer. She could use that.

"Yes," Miranda said. "What was all this about? My family, this planet, capturing a prince just to let him die. Not a smart move in my opinion, unless…"

"Unless?" Rycer said. His smile widened with her eyes. All of the pieces had finally clicked into place.

"Unless this was your end game. You did all of this to get a ship."

"Ding ding ding! We have a winner, folks." Rycer spun all the way around once and then back again to face her.

"Let me get this straight. You started a planetary war to capture our prince, to kill a ship full of people, so you could take said ship to the outer reaches to kill millions of people in the name of… what, exactly?" She egged him on, daring him to keep talking. All she needed was another four, maybe five minutes for the program to take effect.

"In the name of the sanctity of the Holy Mother," he said, his brown eyes alight with the fire of power. He thought he had all of it. All the cards, and it showed. His face glowed with it.

"Who?" Miranda sunk every ounce of her colonial breeding into that one word. He ground his teeth at her.

"The universe, you dimwitted edger," he spat.

"So the universe told you to go and kill a bunch of people," she intoned back. She schooled her face into blank confusion.

He threw up his hands in aggravation. A devious smile crossed his face.

"You poor uneducated mouse," he said. "Your entire life is based on a lie that you readily expand on because no one took the time to teach you different." He began to laugh. A large laugh with the syllables held out a tad bit too long to be natural. The four other rebels with him caught up the laugh until it was more of a chant.

After a time he bent over from laughing so hard. It took another minute before he raised a hand to shut them all up. He looked at her, the fire still alight in his eyes. His gun no longer pointed at Eric. Instead it rested on his knee.

Miranda ducked her head as if in shame, but really it was to hide her looking at her band. Less than a minute to go. She took a long breath and stepped forward and pretended to fall onto Adam. She slipped something into his ears.

"Get off him," Rycer said. Grabbing her by the arm. Miranda got her feet back under her and stood to the side where Rycer pushed her.

"You know what, I think I'm going to enjoy killing you first," he said. He raised his blaster up to her head.

Miranda shrunk back. "Come on, Oscar," she pleaded, even though the little droid couldn't hear her whisper.

An eardrum splitting cry rang out from the com system. Rycer swung his gun around, searching for the source of the noise. He and all his rebel crew fell to their knees clutching their ears. Blood streamed from their noses, eyes, and ears.

Miranda stood over him triumphant. Her ear plugs where tuned against that frequency. So were the ones she'd slipped to Adam in her fake fall. Together they watched as the rebels collapsed to the floor, each one succumbing to the bone shattering whine.

Rycer tried to aim the gun while still holding his hands over his ears as if shooting her would end the noise. He had no idea that Oscar was the one controlling it and that he wasn't even in this room. Miranda kicked the gun easily out of his hand. It slid to her left, underneath the captain's chair.

"How...?" Rycer started to say, but his eyes rolled back in his head and he passed out before finishing the statement.

Miranda smiled.

"Checkmate," she said. All of the rebels were passed out. She made a low whistle and the noise stopped. Adam looked at her with pride in his eyes.

"Remind me to never doubt you again," he said. Miranda let the breath she'd been holding go as she untied his bonds.

"I'm just glad the prick had a vindictive side," she said. They'd been too late to save the captain, but they'd saved Eric. His prone body was on the floor with the rebels.

"Help me carry them to the brig," Miranda asked. Adam nodded. They would be out for hours, but there was no reason to give them the opportunity to escape.

"That sound..." Adam said.

"The Rycor Melody," Miranda said.

Adam eye's widened. "A planetary capture frequency. But how?"

Miranda shrugged, "They teach it in school. As a prince maybe you didn't get the same classes as us poor colonials."

Adam just looked at her. She met his gaze. There were so many other things that needed to be done. The rebels needed to be moved to the brig before they woke up. A rescue shuttle needed to be sent to the planet to get Axel and Fox. A rescue signal needed to be sent to the Imperial forces so that another ship could come and rescue this one. So very many things to do. Miranda didn't know which to do first. After all of that there would be time to mourn. She was lost in her thoughts when a voice broke through the clutter.

"What did I miss?" Eric said. He lifted a now free hand up to scratch his head. Miranda and Adam both broke out in laughter.

Chapter 18

"Here we are."

Miranda looked out the windows of the shuttle at a flat field. Yellow grass grew in patches, breaking up the scene of cracked dirt paths. Miranda took a deep breath and stepped off the end of the shuttle.

"I kept my promise," Eric said, reaching out a hand. She reached hers out and gave it a good shake. Their hands held fast for a second too long. He grasped hers and tightened enough to feel it, but not so tight that it hurt. She slipped her fingers out and saluted; or at least she tried to salute, but it came out more like her limbs flailing around. The slight signs of a smirk played on his lips. He put his helmet back on and turned to board the craft.

She reached out and tugged his sleeve.

"What about the prince?" she asked. "And Axel and everyone else that survived?" After the imperial forces had retrieved the ship, Miranda had remained in the dark. Now their group was reduced back to the first two Ironsides that had come to her rescue at her farm. Had it only been a few days ago? It felt like years all bottled up in blaster fire and exploding ships. If anyone would know what had happened to everyone it would be the team's leader, Eric.

"He was on holiday. The global media got a feed of his retreat to the private planet of Vargon 6."

Miranda whistled. Vargon 6 was a Lux planet with perfect terraforming. Even a shuttle down to planet to spend a day was more than Miranda could make in a year farming.

"Is he really there?" Miranda asked.

"Am I really where?"

Miranda started at the voice. Fox took off his helmet, but it wasn't Fox. If it wasn't for her knowing that the other Ironside was Eri,c she would have sworn she was looking right at him. She still couldn't get over how alike Eric and Adam looked. The same color of hair. The same color of eyes. Even the length of their eyelashes were the same. They had to be universal twins. Just had to be.

Miranda dropped all pretense of propriety and gave him a hug.

"I thought you were Fox," she confessed.

"So Fox gets all the hugs, check," he said, winking at her. "That's what we wanted everyone to think." She buried her face in his armor and breathed in his scent one last time.

"So I'm part of everyone then," she teased.

"Yes, no, I mean..." he stumbled over his words. Miranda smiled. She got a little bit of satisfaction every time she made Adam's smooth exterior slide off in a flustered break. She got really serious on him for a moment.

"I just thought I'd missed my chance to say..." she started. He put a finger to her lips.

"Don't," he said. "This, whatever this is, is a beginning, not an end." Miranda nodded. His finger on her lips sent a shock through her. She stepped back away from the gangplank and the two Ironsides.

"We'll be seeing you soon, Miranda Farmer," Adam said, putting his helmet back on, "very soon indeed."

Miranda watched as the shuttle lifted off and up into the sky.

"Beep bop boop," Oscar said.

"I'm going to miss them too," Miranda responded. Her eyes started to fog up. She bit back the tears. "You heard them. We will see them again. They promised," Miranda reminded Oscar.

"Private Farmer!" a voice called from down the path towards an outcropping of squat buildings. None of them were higher than two stories. They blended in with the dirt at her feet. The only reason she could tell they was there at all was because they didn't have grass growing on them.

"Here," she said. She ran to catch up to the man.

"Well, I guess you are somethin'," he said, looking her over. "Somethin' that needs fixin'. Drop and give me twenty."

Miranda dropped to the ground and started counting.

"One." She smiled.

"Two." She was starting her new life.

"Three." Her left arm gave out, landing her face first in the dust. She tried to lift for four, but her arm wouldn't respond.

"I said give me fifty, Farmer!" the man barked. She struggled back into plank position. Her muscles screamed for relief. It wasn't going to be easy.

"Four," she counted. The sargeant moved on, leaving her there to fulfil his order. Oscar gave her an encouraging beep.

Yes, she would have a lot to keep her busy until she saw her Ironsides again.

Author's Note

Hi! Thank you for reading Imperial Edge. It is the first in a series of books about Miranda and her space adventures. Recently it was brought to my attention that I love mysteries. Every one of my favorite books, TV shows, and Movies have one thing in common. From Scooby Doo to Doctor Who they are all mysteries.

That's the great thing about mystery stories. They aren't stuck in just one genre or type. Sure there are tropes. You can't have a good story if you know everything or are given too many hints. Plus, unmaskings, am I right?

So blending science fiction with a good old who done it is the heart of my new series. I'm calling it Science Fiction Mystery (and no I didn't make this up, it's just not a category on amazon yet).

If you want to know when I'm releasing the next book, sign up for my email list here[1] (https://dl.bookfunnel.com/dnkgzepc6m). You will get a free digital copy of my novella RUN in english along with being added to my email list. This is the list where I send out all my latest news, updates, and book releases.

Thanks,

Celinda

---

1. https://dl.bookfunnel.com/dnkgzepc6m

Preview: Imperial Hilt (Book 2 in Miranda's saga)

Miranda sighed letting go of her aggravation. If she punched her battle buddy there would be no break time on the Seventh day. She wanted her break time. She'd never wanted her break time more than she wanted it now that she was a soldier in the imperial army. Her arms demanded it.

"Ok," the medic was back with a container that looked a lot like her mother's makeup jars. He unscrewed the lid. Miranda scrunched up her nose. The smell hit her hard. She felt like she might pass out.

"A little warning," Farmer said turning his back to her and the medic. The medic shrugged.

"Hazard of the job." the medic stuck two fingers into the jar and took out a large chunk of the paste from inside. He took Miranda's hand and scraped it off onto her palm.

"Strip off your shirt and rub that into all reddened skin." Miranda struggled to comply. Her uniform jacket was hard to get on without holding onto a large handful of goo that was melting at her body temperature. After what felt like forever, she was finally able to escape her jacket and shirt. She wished, not for the first time that things were thought through here. He could have handed her the jar, or told her to strip first. No, shirt off with goop in hand. The imperial way. Her breast band is the only thing between her and the room full of men and women.

At one time she might have cared. She might have worried that someone was looking at her. But not anymore. Everyone here was either too tired, too hurt, or too busy to care about her nakedness. Given that she was all three right then.

She slapped the stinking glob onto her shoulders and neck, down her front, and as far along the back of her neck and shoulders that she could reach. She had to get a second handful. There was so much skin.

"Here," the Medic said when he noticed that she was out of the paste.

"I need to use the bathroom," Farmer said standing up from the cot.

"Through the double doors on the left," the medic said handing Miranda a third scoop for her arms. Farmer nodded and headed down the hall. She wasn't supposed to ever separate from her battle buddy, but Miranda was glad to see him go. She watched the doors swing shut.

Too late she asked, "Should I go with him?"

"It's fine," the medic said. "Once you are on the ward you don't have to stick that close," he gave her a wink as he scraped the last of the medication from the container.

"Here," he said, "finish putting this on your back."

He tossed the jar in a trash can to the left of the bed. Miranda hoped that if she had to stay here for long the smell would dissipate given showers weren't for two more days.

The medic pulled a long string of key cards out of his pocket and tapped one against the smooth metal stand to the right of the bed. A drawer popped out exposing an array of bandages in all shapes and sizes. He got to work cutting and arranging them over the areas she'd lathered with the goo.

"You can put your shirt on now," he said. She rubbed the last of the medicine into her hands before reaching for her military issued shirt. The brown fabric slid over her bandaged back and shoulders, the sting already dissipating.

"No showers for two day," the medic said, handing her a sheet of instructions. There were other things like a restriction on night patrols and staying out of the sun for twenty four hours. Miranda nodded.

"Give that to your drill instructor," he said, "stay here until your buddy comes back then you may return to duty." The medic got up off the bed and turned his back to her to help the next patient.

It wasn't until that moment that she realised she hadn't read his name plate. She hit her head against her palm. All soldiers wore name plates. It made calling everyone something easier for a person like her. And she hadn't even taken the time to look.

"Oh well," she thought, "next time." She went to lay back on the bed when her battle buddy Farmer chased through the double doors into the room.

"Dead," he screamed. Every head in the room turned towards her battle buddy.

"He's dead!" he screamed again.

Made in the USA
Middletown, DE
28 March 2020